PEEK A BOO I SEE YOU

WILLOW ROSE

BOOKS BY THE AUTHOR

HARRY HUNTER MYSTERY SERIES

- ALL THE GOOD GIRLS
- RUN GIRL RUN
- NO OTHER WAY
- NEVER WALK ALONE

MARY MILLS MYSTERY SERIES

- WHAT HURTS THE MOST
- YOU CAN RUN
- YOU CAN'T HIDE
- CAREFUL LITTLE EYES

EVA RAE THOMAS MYSTERY SERIES

- DON'T LIE TO ME
- WHAT YOU DID
- NEVER EVER
- SAY YOU LOVE ME
- LET ME GO
- IT'S NOT OVER
- NOT DEAD YET
- TO DIE FOR

EMMA FROST SERIES

- ITSY BITSY SPIDER
- MISS DOLLY HAD A DOLLY

- Run, Run as Fast as You Can
- Cross Your Heart and Hope to Die
- Peek-a-Boo I See You
- Tweedledum and Tweedledee
- Easy as One, Two, Three
- There's No Place like Home
- Slenderman
- Where the Wild Roses Grow
- Waltzing Mathilda
- Drip Drop Dead
- Black Frost

JACK RYDER SERIES

- Hit the Road Jack
- Slip out the Back Jack
- The House that Jack Built
- Black Jack
- Girl Next Door
- Her Final Word
- Don't Tell

REBEKKA FRANCK SERIES

- One, Two...He is Coming for You
- Three, Four...Better Lock Your Door
- Five, Six...Grab your Crucifix
- Seven, Eight...Gonna Stay up Late
- Nine, Ten...Never Sleep Again
- Eleven, Twelve...Dig and Delve
- Thirteen, Fourteen...Little Boy Unseen
- Better Not Cry
- Ten Little Girls
- It Ends Here

MYSTERY/THRILLER/HORROR NOVELS

- Sorry Can't Save You
- In One Fell Swoop
- Umbrella Man
- Blackbird Fly
- To Hell in a Handbasket
- Edwina

HORROR SHORT-STORIES

- Mommy Dearest
- The Bird
- Better watch out
- Eenie, Meenie
- Rock-a-Bye Baby
- Nibble, Nibble, Crunch
- Humpty Dumpty
- Chain Letter

PARANORMAL SUSPENSE/ROMANCE NOVELS

- In Cold Blood
- The Surge
- Girl Divided

THE VAMPIRES OF SHADOW HILLS SERIES

- Flesh and Blood
- Blood and Fire
- Fire and Beauty
- Beauty and Beasts
- Beasts and Magic
- Magic and Witchcraft

- Witchcraft and War
- War and Order
- Order and Chaos
- Chaos and Courage

THE AFTERLIFE SERIES

- Beyond
- Serenity
- Endurance
- Courageous

THE WOLFBOY CHRONICLES

- A Gypsy Song
- I am WOLF

DAUGHTERS OF THE JAGUAR

- Savage
- Broken

Peek-a-boo, I see you—boo boo!
    Peek-a-boo, do you see me? Boo boo!
    Peek-a-boo, I see you—boo boo!
    It's fun playing peek-a-boo with you.
    It's fun playing peek-a-boo—with you.

CHILDREN'S SONG WRITTEN BY DENISA
SENOVSKY

PROLOGUE
FEBRUARY 2014

They called her Susie Sunshine. Mostly because she was always so entertaining and joyful. On the good days that was. That was when everybody loved her and enjoyed being around her.

Susie opened her eyes and stared at the white ceiling, wondering if this was one of those days or if it was one of the others. One of the black ones where she had no energy for anything. On those days, all she wanted was to be left alone. She especially didn't want to see her mother, who always stopped by around noon to make sure Susie was out of bed and that she had taken her medicine. But Susie had cheated the last couple of days. She did that sometimes. Stopped taking her medicine. Just for a couple of days usually. Just to lose a couple of pounds. The medicine made her eat more and made her gain weight. A lot of weight. Susie was tired of being fat. So, that was why she sometimes cheated on her meds.

But this time, it was different. This time it hadn't happened on purpose. This time, she actually hadn't been able to find her medicine for at least a week now. She simply couldn't remember where she had put the bottle. She didn't want to admit it to her mother, who would go berserk if she knew. She would blame her for cheating on her medicine and immediately admit her to the hospital again. Susie really didn't want that, so she kept it to herself and just hoped and prayed that this would be one of the good days. One of those where she had tons of energy and hardly needed any sleep at all.

Those days her doctor referred to as the *manic* days.

Those were the best. And Susie had missed them. When she had her manic days, anything was possible. She even liked herself and she was funny and told jokes that made people like her. But then, when the depressive days arrived - which they always did at some point - no one understood where the funny girl had gone. They all wanted their clown back.

Susie lifted her head and looked out the window, pulling the curtains aside. The sun was shining. It was rare at this time of year and she closed her eyes as the rays of the sun hit her face through the glass. She put the palm of her hand to the glass and felt how cold it was. It had snowed while she was sleeping and the yard belonging to her small apartment on the first floor that the county had provided for her, was covered in white. The neighbor's daughter was playing outside, making a huge snowman. Her mother watched her from the window with a cigarette in her mouth. Susie knew it was hard on the neighbor to have her daughter visiting. She lived with her father and only came twice a month, so as not to overburden the mother. Susie smiled at the sight of the girl and felt like jumping out the window into the snow and playing with her.

Susie burst into laughter. It was one of the good days. It had been for almost the entire week now. Maybe the depression wouldn't come this time around? Maybe it was possible for her to stay happy forever and ever? In her mind, anything could happen right now. She could possibly even learn how to fly.

Susie jumped out of the bed feeling ecstatic. She stretched her hands in the air to embrace the beautiful morning. A neighbor walking by her window looked in and seemed perplexed by her nakedness in the window. Susie laughed and shook her body, forcing her big breasts to dangle back and forth.

The man ran away. Susie laughed again. She felt like running after the guy and bringing him back to her place. It was always like that on the good days. Her sex drive went haywire. She craved sex and often ended up with the strangest types.

Susie laughed again and held a hand to her belly. Oh what a wonderful day this was. She felt like going outside, maybe visiting her neighbor who was staring anxiously at her daughter through the window. Maybe cheer her up a little? Lord knows she could use some cheering up and Susie was in a perfect mood for just that. She felt almost invincible.

How beautiful the world is today. I feel like singing and danc-ing. I feel such love for everyone and want to tell them how much I love them. Why do they all look so sad when they pass my window? I don't understand why they're not all playing in the beautiful snow?

Susie chuckled and looked at the girl playing, then she decided to run outside, not thinking for one second about the fact that she was still naked.

With a huge smile, Susie jumped out the door and screamed as she threw herself in a pile of freezing snow. Laughing mani-cally, she rolled around. She didn't even notice the young girl's small shriek, nor the fact that she rushed back to her mother's apartment shaking and trembling with fear. No, Susie laughed and rolled in the snow like it was the most natural thing in the world.

Meanwhile, the neighbors closed their curtains and moved away from the windows, knowing that it wouldn't be long before the police arrived and Susie would be admitted to the psychiatric ward once again. They had seen her like this many times before and didn't want to get involved.

Susie didn't stop laughing until the moment a hand was

reached down towards her and she grabbed it. In front of her stood a person dressed in a long black coat.

Susie smiled.

"You'll catch a cold," the person said.

Susie answered with another carefree laugh.

"Not me," she said. Then she repeated it again and again like a four-year-old would do. "Not me, not me, not me."

"You don't get cold?" the person in the long coat asked.

Susie giggled and shook her head. "No! Not me. I'm invincible. I can do anything. Can't you see?"

"I do see," the person said. "And I do believe you."

Clouds had gathered in the sky and covered the sun. Now it was starting to snow again. Susie threw her head back and stuck her tongue out. Several snowflakes landed on it and melted. It made her laugh again.

"You're just having fun, aren't you?" the person in the coat asked.

Susie closed her mouth and looked at the person in front of her. "I *am* having fun. I really am. I think I'll stay out here all day. Oh no, maybe I should go skiing. Do you want to come? Do you want to go skiing with me?" she asked with wide-open eyes.

"I'm afraid I'm not much of a skier," the person answered. "Plus I don't have any skis. Do you?"

"I'll just go anyway. I don't need any skis," she said with a grin.

"Of course you don't. 'Cause you can do anything, can't you?" the person asked with a smile.

"Well yes. You are right. I can do anything."

"Can you also fly?"

Susie froze. Then she nodded slowly. "Yes. Yes I can. How did you know that?"

The person shrugged. "Took a wild guess. You know I have always dreamed of learning how to fly. Could you show me?"

Susie giggled. She felt so happy at this moment in her life and she never wanted it to go away. She loved this strange person in the black coat and beanie standing in front of her so much right now. And, of course, she would like to help him learn how to fly. Everyone should learn how to fly like the birds.

"Yes," she said. "Of course I'll show you, come."

She grabbed his coat and pulled him. She knew exactly where she was going to show him. She walked back into the building and into the elevator where she pushed the button for the fifth floor. The person followed her and stepped in with her. Susie giggled all the way up, thinking about how wonderful it was going to be to finally have someone to fly with. It could be so lonesome up there among the birds. At least that was what she thought. Suddenly, she couldn't remember. But she knew she had done this before. She definitely had. Hadn't she? Yes. Yes, she had. Many times. She could still hear her father's words to her:

Susie Sunshine shines in the sky like diamonds.

The elevator stopped and they went out. Susie showed the way to the stairs leading to the roof. She had been up there many times before to fly and knew how to get up there, even if it was locked. She knew a trick to unlock the door and now she showed her new friend, using one of his credit cards.

The door opened and Susie went outside on the roof. With great confidence, she walked towards the edge and looked back at the person who was smiling and nodding.

"I'll go first, then you follow," Susie said with a grin. "Make sure you watch me closely first to see how to do it."

"Sure," the person said.

Susie climbed up on the railing, bent her knees, and jumped. She felt the cold air against her skin as she skyrocketed through the air. She screamed with joy and flapped her arms wildly.

1

APRIL 2000

Samuel was the cutest little boy. His mother especially thought so. Alexandra Holm was a woman in her mid-thirties when she had him and he was exactly like the child she had always wanted. He had the cutest chubby cheeks, the bluest of eyes and blondest of hair. He was gorgeous and everyone told Alexandra so when they saw him.

Alexandra thought about the day when she had first held him in her arms as she watched him blow out the candles on his cake for his four-year birthday. These had been the best four years of her life. Her husband Poul had thought so too and now they were exchanging loving glances as the boy shrieked with joy over being able to blow out all the candles at once.

"That's my boy," Alexandra said, and cut a piece of the cake and put it on the boy's plate. The piece tipped over on the plate.

"Moom," the boy whined, annoyed.

"Sorry," she said with a smile and flipped it upright again. She placed the plate in front of him. "There. Now it's perfect."

"Say cheese," Poul said, and took a picture of Samuel.

Samuel didn't look up.

"Samuel, look at me," Poul said.

Still, the boy didn't react.

"Samuel, look at your dad," Alexandra said.

"I don't want to," Samuel replied, then dug his fingers deep into the cake.

Alexandra's mother gasped. She was sitting next to Poul's parents at the table. "Alexandra," her mother said, with a condemning tone. "You can't let him do that."

"Samuel, use your spoon," Alexandra said, feeling very self-conscious.

It had been hard becoming a mother, she thought. Harder than expected. Especially the disciplining part had become increasingly harder and harder for her. She wasn't tough enough on the boy, her own mother kept telling her that when Samuel acted out.

"Boys need discipline," she would say. "They need consistency; they need to know right from wrong at a very early age. And most importantly, they need to know who is in charge. Don't let him think he's in control, or he'll end up controlling everything in just a few years."

But for someone like Alexandra, it was hard to be tough on her little boy, who she adored so much. She had tried to become pregnant for more than eight years, so finally receiving a child was a gift that needed to be cherished. She couldn't find it in her heart to be angry at the boy and, especially, not to raise her voice at him.

"Please, Samuel. Use your spoon to eat with," she repeated, when he didn't listen. She looked at her mother, who stared at her with contempt. Alexandra blushed and picked up the spoon. She tried to hand it to him.

"Samuel, use the spoon, please."

The boy laughed and kept eating with his fingers. Alexandra felt discouraged. Wasn't it, after all, his birthday? Wasn't he supposed to have fun and do as he pleased for once?

Alexandra looked at Poul who shrugged. Alexandra was torn inside. She wanted to discipline the boy, yet she wanted him to have fun on his birthday and, if that meant eating his cake with his fingers, then shouldn't he be allowed to?

"Alexandra," her mother said, with a harsh tone. "He really shouldn't..."

"I know, Mom. I know," she interrupted her. She turned towards her son. "Samuel, please use your spoon," she repeated, more firmly than she liked to.

The boy stopped eating and looked up at his mother. What she saw in his eyes scared her more than anything. Those delightful blue eyes that she loved so dearly suddenly turned almost black. Alexandra gasped.

Samuel let out an ear-piercing scream before he picked up the cake from his plate and started throwing it at his mother. When there was no more cake, he picked up the spoon and threw it at her, then the plate. Alexandra whimpered and drew backwards, while Poul looked at the scene with nothing but apathy.

"Samuel. Stop it immediately," Alexandra's mother yelled at the boy.

But the boy didn't stop. His tantrum continued. He jumped down from his chair and ran towards his mother, hitting his fists into her stomach. Alexandra whimpered and cried. She held his shoulders to hold him back, but the boy seemed, suddenly, to possess inhuman strength and managed to get free. He hit her again and again and Alexandra cried in despair.

"Please, sweet Samuel. Please stop."

"Poul, do something," Alexandra's mother said.

Poul looked at her like he didn't understand.

"Take the boy to his room," her mother said.

Poul put the camera down carefully then stormed towards them, grabbed the boy around the waist and, while Samuel was kicking and screaming, he carried him up the stairs and put him in his room. Alexandra staggered backwards and landed on the couch. Whimpering, she sat down while listening with terror to her son screaming and yelling from his room upstairs, banging and kicking the door.

2

FEBRUARY 2014

I was staring at the letter on the kitchen table in front of me like I had been for the last hour, wondering whether I should open it or not.

The big white envelope seemed to be mocking me. Could I open it and not care what the result was? Could I not open it and go around uncertain about the result for the rest of my life?

I sipped my coffee and took another piece of chocolate. I had eaten almost an entire package of my favorite Marabou-chocolate with licorice since I had emptied the mailbox that same morning after the kids had taken off to school.

"It was going to happen one time or another, Emma," I told myself. "The result was going to come. You knew this. You asked for it. You can't keep going on as if everything is the same."

I inhaled deeply, picked up the envelope and looked at it. My daughter's name on the front seemed so huge, like it was yelling at me to open it.

I didn't want to. I really didn't want to know the truth about my daughter's father. I had contacted Erik Gundtofte and told him to go to a lab in Copenhagen and leave a sample for them to examine.

I sent them hair from my daughter's brush to take a DNA sample from and have them compare them. Now they had the result and I was terrified of the truth.

Maybe it won't show anything. He is, after all, only one out of many that could be Maya's father. What are the chances? Just open it, you coward, and get it over with.

I shrugged and turned the envelope over with the intention of finally opening it when, suddenly, the doorbell rang.

"No, not now!" I mumbled. "Go away."

I stared at the half-opened envelope. My heart was racing. Part of me wanted to be disturbed, wanted to have to postpone it, while the other half wanted to get it over with.

The doorbell rang again and I got up. I hid the letter in a drawer, then went for the door. Thinking it was maybe a package of clothes that Maya had ordered, I opened the door expecting to find my mailman, but it wasn't him.

"Hi, honey."

I was startled. Almost in shock.

"Mom?"

The woman standing outside looked like my mother, except she looked ten years younger.

"You lost weight," I said.

"Almost fifty pounds," she said with a smile. She turned her body in the leather jacket and leather pants. "Looking good, right?"

"Did you do something to your face?" I asked.

It looked like she tried not to smile, but her expression remained the same. "Got a facelift and some Botox. You like it?"

I didn't know what to say. To be honest, she looked terrible. Not that it wasn't nicely done, she just didn't look like my mother.

"Can I come inside?" she asked.

"Of course," I said and spotted the three huge Louis Vuitton suitcases behind her. She left them there and entered my house.

"What about the...?" I asked, but she was gone.

I stared at the three suitcases that had to have cost at least two-thousand Euros each. They probably wouldn't last long in my yard, so I grabbed one and carried it inside.

After getting all three of them inside my hallway, I closed the door and walked to the kitchen where I found my mother sitting at the table, still looking like she was the happiest person on earth. The only thing that gave her away was a small tear that had escaped the corner of her eye and now rolled down her cheek.

"What are you doing here, Mom? Why aren't you in Spain with that Pablo-guy?"

My mother sniffled and looked at me. She was still smiling from ear to ear, which made her really creepy to look at, while another tear rolled down her cheek.

"Pedro," she corrected me. "Pedro left me."

3

FEBRUARY 2014

I poured my mother some coffee and we sat at the kitchen table while drinking it. I found some candy in a drawer and put it in a bowl. My mother didn't touch it, while I couldn't keep my fingers out of it. I felt highly uncomfortable in this situation and that always made me eat.

"So, what happened, Mom?" I asked with my mouth filled with salty fish, my favorite licorice.

"He found someone else, the bastard," she said. "Guess he finally got tired of being with someone ten years older than him."

She looked at me while I took another piece of licorice. "I don't understand how you can eat that garbage," she added, and made me feel even more uncomfortable. "The sugar and salt is horrible for your skin, sweetie. If you keep this up, you'll end up looking old by next week. Not to mention what it does for your waist. You really should think more about your health, Emma. You've gained weight since I saw you last. You're young and still look good, but that won't last, dear, and then there'll be nothing left but the extra kilos and... well, you know...You'll be old and alone. Like me."

Her comments made me feel insecure and I grabbed an extra handful candy to soothe my emotions. "I don't care," I said.

My mother sipped her coffee that she had taken black since I didn't have any of the skinny almond milk that she usually used. I stared at her, wondering how long she thought she was going to stay here. I had hardly seen her in the past four years, since she suddenly left my dad for her Spanish adventure with Pedro. I had visited her twice and felt like I was visiting a stranger. Now I had the same feeling again. This woman in my kitchen didn't resemble much of the mother I had grown up with. The mother I had known loved my dad and the life they had together. She took care of me and always made sure the house looked impeccable. Sure, she had a few extra kilos and wrinkles that showed she had lived a full life taking care of her family, but she had been happy. And I had at least been able to see it on her face if she wasn't. Now, I didn't know. She was crying, I saw tears now and then in her eyes, but her face remained the same. It was constantly smiling. To be honest, it creeped me out.

"So...," I said. "So...what are you going to do now?"

"Well, what are my options? He was the one with all the money. We aren't married so I don't get a thing, do I?"

I sipped my coffee, not liking where this was going. "Nope," I said and grabbed another licorice.

"Of course I don't. Four years I put into that relationship and then he goes off and finds someone else. A flight attendant from one of his many business trips, the pig. You should see her, Emma. She is gorgeous. I tell you the legs on that girl...I can't blame him, really. Can't say I didn't see it coming with the way my body is deteriorating."

"Well, maybe there is supposed to be more to a relationship than just one's looks," I said. "Especially when you reach a certain age."

"What is that supposed to mean? Did you just call me old?" my mother said.

I tilted my head. "Mom, you are old. I'm sorry to be the one to tell you, but you're almost seventy. That's a nice age, but it's not young anymore. You're a beautiful woman, but to be frank, you've come to look kind of scary with all the work you've had done. I can hardly recognize you anymore. I really never got why you'd ever run away with that Pablo-guy anyway. I especially don't understand how you could do it to Dad, who loves you and still insists on protecting you whenever I say anything bad. That's real love, Mom. Do you have any idea how sad he was when you left? He hardly ate or slept for months. He was so confused and sad, while you were down there having a blast in the sun. Not that I don't want you to have fun, I do, but you left a man who truly loved you. There, I said it."

My mother stared at me with a smiling face, but I knew she wasn't happy. She never took the truth well. I didn't care anymore. I had been wanting to say this to her for years. Now I had.

"Do you want some candy?" I asked, and pushed the bowl closer to her. I laughed when I noticed the fear in her eyes, as if the candy was going to attack her. "Come on, Mom. How long has it been since you last had a piece of candy? Live a little."

My mom chuckled. Then she shrugged. "Guess one piece wouldn't hurt."

"There you go, Mom," I said, and watched as she picked one up, put it in her mouth and started chewing. My mother closed her eyes.

"Oh my. I had completely forgotten how wonderful licorice tastes," she said, with a deep groan.

"I know. Why would you cheat yourself out of anything good in life?" I asked. "We only get this short time on earth and I intend to enjoy it while it lasts."

My mom looked at the bowl of candy. I pushed it closer. "Have another one," I said. "I'll make us some more coffee."

I got up from my chair and put on another pot of coffee, while my mother took another piece of candy.

"So, tell me about that policeman of yours," she said with a chuckle.

"Morten?"

"Yes, you told me about him the last time I called. In December, I think it was."

"What's to tell? He's nice. Not very handsome, but that doesn't matter. He's good to me. I like him."

"I can tell you like him," my mother said.

I felt slightly uncomfortable again. It felt strange to be talking to my mother like this. She hadn't seemed interested in my life at all the last several years and it was only because I told her stuff about myself and the children that she knew anything at all. Why all this interest all of a sudden? I couldn't quite grasp it or contain it. It felt strange. I didn't know if I even wanted her in my life again or to share details about my life with her.

The coffee was done and I poured us some more, then sat down and looked at my mother again. "So what are you going to do, Mom?"

She exhaled. "I guess I'll stay with you for a little while?"

I almost choked on my coffee. I kind of knew it was coming with the suitcases and all, but it still startled me. "Really?" I said with a shrill voice.

"Well you're all I've got now, right? You and the kids. I think it's about time they spend some time with their grandmother. Then you can go out with that Morten-guy of yours."

I stared at my mother in disbelief. Why was she saying these things? Did she want something from me? There had to be an alternate motive or something. My mother never wanted to just hang out with my children. Especially not with Victor who could be very difficult to handle.

"Don't you want that?" she asked. "To be able to spend more time with Morten?"

"Well yes, I guess I do."

My cell phone vibrated on the kitchen table. I looked at the display, then back at my mother. "Speaking of ... " I said, and took it. "Morten? I thought you were at work all day?"

"I am," he said. His voice was very serious. My heart dropped. A million thoughts ran through my head. Had something happened to Maya at school? Or to Victor?

"What's going on?" I asked.

"We found a body outside City Hall. I need you to come down immediately."

4

JULY 2001

It was a nice, warm summer Saturday and Alexandra had planned a day at the beach. She loved living on the island of Fanoe with its wide sandy beaches...especially in the summertime. They didn't have much money and couldn't afford to go on vacation, but they didn't need it since they had - in her opinion - the best beaches in the world within walking distance.

Alexandra was whistling while packing a lunch basket and finding towels and beach toys for Samuel to play with. As a teacher, Alexandra had five weeks off in the summertime, but Poul had just started his own auto repair shop, so he had to work all summer. So, it was only going to be the two of them. Up until now, it had been good. Alexandra had spent extra time with Samuel, giving him the extra amount of attention that his doctor had told her he needed.

The tantrum at his four-year birthday party hadn't been his last. But Alexandra knew he didn't mean to be bad. After trashing his entire room and breaking everything inside of it that was breakable, he had been so remorseful it almost hurt Alexandra. He had told her how sorry he was and held her tightly, crying. Weeks had passed where he had been the most delightful child, helping Alexandra out with almost everything and always telling her how much he loved her and that she was the best mother in the entire world. He had been the angel that Alexandra always knew he was, up until two months later when Alexandra had told him to clean up his Legos from the living room floor. That was when he had lost it again. And this time, his tantrum seemed even stronger than the first time. Alexandra had been alone with him at the time and had not known what to do. So, she had left him alone and run up the stairs and closed the door to her bedroom while the boy destroyed their living room. The rage ended with him punching a hole in the wall, then he went quiet. When Alexandra came down, she found him sitting on the floor crying, his hand bleeding.

So, she took him to the doctor. She told the doctor about the tantrum and rage and the doctor explained to her that Samuel was a very passionate boy and maybe a little more intense and that he probably needed a lot more attention from his mother than other children.

"Tantrums are normal in a five-year old. He'll grow out of it, don't worry."

But it still hadn't gotten any better. In his preschool, they complained that Samuel pulled the girls' hair and threw stuff around when he got angry. Alexandra made all kinds of excuses and told them she would get the boy under control, but so far, she still didn't know how to handle him once he got into that zone. It was like he was unreachable. Poul didn't want to talk about it. He had enough trouble at work, he would say.

"You're his mother. You figure it out."

So now, Alexandra had decided to spend the entire summer doing nothing but giving her boy a lot of attention. She planned activities for them to do every day and, so far, she had avoided any bad confrontations and tantrums.

She exhaled deeply and closed the basket containing the sandwiches, hoping and praying that this was going to be one of the good days as well.

"Samuel?" she called. "Are you ready? I put your swim shorts out for you. Did you put them on?"

There was no answer, so Alexandra put the basket down and walked up the stairs. The door to Samuel's room was ajar and she pushed it open. She found him sitting on the carpet inside with the swim pants in his hand.

Alexandra exhaled, relieved. "Do you need help?" she asked and kneeled next to him.

He didn't react. He stared into the air without moving.

"Samuel?"

Samuel turned his head and stared at his mother with pitch-black eyes. Alexandra gasped and drew backwards.

"I told you...I...don't...like...these...SHORTS!"

Alexandra shook her head. "You never said that...but...you don't have to wear them, Samuel. We can find another pair." Alexandra got up and opened a drawer, then frantically searched for another pair and found them. She pulled them out. "See. You have these as well. They're nice, right?"

But it was too late. Samuel had that look in his eyes that Alexandra had come to know frighteningly well.

"I don't want to wear those either," he said. "I HATE swim shorts. I HATE the beach."

"No you don't, sweetie. You love the beach, remember? We'll get to build a sandcastle and maybe play soccer?"

Samuel was breathing heavily now and Alexandra had a feeling it was too late. No words were able to calm him down now. She had seen that look in his eyes before. But to her surprise, Samuel remained calm. He didn't throw anything at her or even scream. Instead, he simply looked at her with his pitch-black eyes and said:

"Mom, I love you, and I don't want to hurt you, but some days, I have to."

With utter terror in her eyes, Alexandra drew backwards, then stormed out of the room and into her own bedroom where she stayed until Poul came home.

5

FEBRUARY 2014

M y mother stayed at the house while I drove towards City Hall with my heart pounding in my throat. Morten hadn't told me much on the phone and, to be frank, I was completely freaked out by the whole thing.

Why did he need me to come down? They found a body, but what did that have to do with me?

I turned into the parking lot in front of City Hall where the island's police car was parked. I parked mine next to it. I spotted Morten and another officer on the other side of the police tape. A small flock of people had gathered to watch. I walked past them and Morten spotted me. He ran to greet me. I followed him closer to the scene, my eyes fixated on the body on the tiles that was covered with a white blanket.

Is it someone I know since they want me down here? It couldn't be any of my children since he would have told me, wouldn't he? Or is he bracing himself right now to tell me? Is he? Oh God, don't let him be!

"You're scaring me here," I said. "Tell me right away. Is it any of my children? Is it my dad? I tried to call him all the way down here, but he didn't answer his phone."

"Sorry," Morten answered. "How insensitive of me. It's no one from your family. As a matter of fact, we haven't quite figured out who she is yet, so don't worry about that."

I exhaled, relieved, and my heart calmed slightly. "Oh good," I said. "But why am I here, then?"

"I have to show you this. That's why I couldn't tell you on the phone," Morten said and grabbed the blanket. He pulled it and I braced myself for what I was about to see.

"This woman was found here this morning when the clerk came to open up City Hall at eight. She was lying just the way you see her here in front of the main entrance, blocking it so no one could enter without seeing her."

I looked down at the body and felt nauseated.

"Her head has been decapitated," Morten continued, "and the back of her head suffered a trauma of some sort. Looks like a blow from a fall. I've seen something similar before in another case, but the forensics will clear that up for us when they arrive from Copenhagen."

"I see all that," I said, feeling confused. "But why...What does this have to do with me?"

Morten nodded slowly. He reached down and grabbed the body and turned it around, while the head remained in its place.

"We didn't know it had anything to do with you until we started examining her and found this," he said, and turned her naked body all the way around to show me the back of it.

I gasped. Carved into the skin was a series of letters spelling a message:

PEEK-A-BOO, EMMA FROST

Startled, I pulled backwards, covering my mouth with my hand. "What...what the hell is that?"

Morten shrugged with a sigh. "I don't know. It looks like someone wants your attention."

I shook my head in distrust. "But...but...What is this? I mean who would do such a horrible thing?"

Morten covered the body with the blanket, then put a hand on my shoulder. "I don't know, Emma. But it looks like you're going to be a part of figuring that out, whether you like it or not. We're going to need your help. It might just be some psycho who likes your books or something. I mean you have become quite the name in this country and with fame comes a whole lot of stuff that you never asked for."

"I know...I know. I'm just...I don't understand. I don't know this woman. I've never seen her before in my life."

"Good, at least we've established that. That was kind of the reason I brought you down here. I thought you might know her."

"I really don't."

"Okay," Morten said. "Then you're free to go back home. I have to wait for the forensic team to come and then secure the area for anything we can use. We found a couple of shoeprints over there that I hope will give us a clue."

I was about to leave when something struck me. "Didn't the body strike you as odd," I said.

"What do you mean? She's been decapitated and a message has been carved into her back, so yes, but other than that?"

"Yes," I said and walked closer. I swallowed hard before grabbing the blanket and pulling it away again. "Look," I said and pointed.

"What am I looking at?"

"The head doesn't seem to quite fit the body, does it?"

"What do you mean?"

"The body is very slim and fit, but her face is quite round and somehow seems way too big for that tiny body."

Morten nodded and touched his face. "I believe you're right," he said pensively. "It does look strange."

"If you ask me, it's been put together like this. I think you have *two* dead women. The question is...where is the rest of them?"

6

FEBRUARY 2014

PEEK-A-BOO **EMMA FROST?**

I kept repeating the message to myself in the car on my way back. Part of me wondered if this was all some stupid dream. This entire morning had been so surreal, I had no idea how to grasp it. It was all a little too much. I understood what Morten said with me being a name and all and it was true. I had written four books by now and was trying to finish my fifth about the crazy stay at Hotel Brinkloev, but it kept giving me problems because I wanted to leave all the stuff out about my daughter. I wondered if I should just kill the book and start something new, since I was tired of the story and it kept nagging me with what I had discovered up there. After all, not everything I experienced had to be a book. That was what Maya always told me, but I couldn't help it. It was my way of dealing with all that had happened to me during the last couple of years. Plus, I made a lot of money on the books, now that I had sold the rights to several other European countries. I was making enough for me to take a few years off if I wanted to.

But I didn't like the idea that this killing had something to do with me. Why me, of all people?

I parked the car in the driveway in front of my grandmother's old house and looked at the facade before I went in. It really needed a renovation.

Maybe that should be your spring project instead of writing another book?

I walked into the kitchen and found my mother sitting where I'd left her with a laptop on the table.

"Hi, honey," she said, and looked up. "Oh my, you look terrible. I never noticed how pale you are. You need to get out more in the fresh air or travel places. Get some sun and vitamin D."

I had no idea what to say to this woman. I felt exhausted and couldn't cope with her and her sudden pretended interest in me.

"I...I think I'll go upstairs for a little while," I said.

"Do that, sweetheart. I have a lot of e-mails to answer anyway. Take a nap. Maybe you're just tired."

"Maybe."

I walked up the stairs and went into my bedroom where I threw myself on the bed. I felt like crying, but no tears came. I think I was in some state of shock. I didn't know what to call it. I just felt so incredibly tired.

So naturally, I fell asleep and didn't wake up until it was almost dark outside. I gasped and looked out the window at the dusk. Then, I opened my eyes wide and jumped out of the bed.

"The kids!"

I rushed down the stairs, feeling horrible for not being there when they got home. I was always there to greet them. I almost always baked something for them. They had to be so sad.

At least I thought so until I heard Maya's laughter coming from the kitchen. I walked in and found her sitting at the table with a cup in her hand. Next to her sat my mother. They looked chummy and, somehow, that annoyed me more than anything.

"Hi, Mom," Maya said.

"Where is your brother?"

"He's in the yard playing," my mother said. "He didn't say

much, but went straight out there after he came home. Maya here tells me he likes to play out there. That's good. Gets a lot of fresh air and exercise."

"He's all right, Mom," Maya said. "I checked on him not long ago. He's wearing his warm snowsuit and everything. I made sure of that."

I inhaled sharply. "Well, that's good. But I better get him inside now. It's getting dark."

"Can't he tell it's getting dark and figure out to come inside on his own?" My mother asked with a scoff. "I mean, he is eight years old now, right? He should know when it's time to come back in."

I closed my eyes and calmed myself down to not answer her too harshly. "No, Mom, he doesn't know when it's time to come back inside. When he's in a world of his own, he doesn't sense his surroundings. If I don't get him inside, he'll stay out there all night. He's not like other kids; he doesn't think of consequences."

"That sounds like nonsense to me," she said. "You're just being overprotective. No good has ever come from that."

I drew in a deep breath, then walked out of the kitchen without answering her. I found Victor in the middle of the yard talking to the tallest of the birch trees.

"Victor! It's time to come back in, buddy. It's getting dark."

He didn't answer. I was used to that. "Victor? Buddy?"

He nodded and looked at the tree. "I'll make sure to ask her," he said, right before he came towards me and walked right past me.

I caught up with him. "Hi, buddy. How was your day at school?"

"Bad," he said. "You know it was. It always is. Why do I have to say the same thing every day? Why do you ask the same thing every day? It doesn't make any sense. People spend way too much time talking about stuff that doesn't matter."

"But it matters to me, Victor. I really want to know how your day was. Maybe I secretly hope that it will be good one of these days."

Victor didn't say anything. He kept walking towards the porch.

"So, what did you have to ask whom?" I said.

"What?" he asked, as we reached the porch and I told him to take his muddy shoes off.

"You told the tree you would ask someone something, what was that? Who was it?"

"You," he said. Victor lifted his eyes and looked into mine, something he rarely did. Only if what he had to tell me was important.

"He asked me if you liked to play *Hide and Go Seek*."

Victor turned around and walked inside the house, leaving muddy prints all over the wooden planks with his dirty socks.

"Wait, Victor," I said and stormed after him. "What did the tree mean by that?" I asked and suddenly heard how silly of a sentence that was. But Victor had a way of knowing things and I had reached a point where I couldn't ignore it anymore. I didn't dare to. "What do you think it meant?"

But Victor didn't answer. He kept walking towards the kitchen and disappeared through the door. I followed him, but stopped when my phone vibrated in my pocket. I took it out and saw Morten's name on the display.

"Still working, huh?" I asked, as I answered.

"Yes. This is going to be late. I'll sleep at my own place since I have to get up early, if that's alright with you?"

I was disappointed, but at the same time, relieved. I hadn't told him about my mother showing up all of a sudden and I wasn't prepared for him to meet her just yet.

"Sure. We'll see each other tomorrow night instead. Any news on the identity of the woman?"

"You were right. The head didn't belong to the body. The face has been identified as a woman named Susie Larsen. She was twenty-six years old and living in these condos outside of town where the county places a lot of psychiatric patients. She was bipolar and disappeared three days ago. Her mother reported her missing. She was afraid she had forgotten to take her medicine and usually that makes her lose the sense of reality. Last time she disappeared, we picked her up in an apartment where she had barged in on some people who didn't know her. We found her sitting naked in the open window while singing. So naturally, the mother was concerned about what Susie had come up with this time. I am on my way to her house now to tell her what we've found."

"That's a tough one, huh?"

Morten breathed in the phone. "It is. Especially since I don't have much to tell her. I don't know how she died. We haven't even discovered the rest of her body yet. We probably can't say anything about the cause of death before we find it."

"Well...good luck. Let me know how it went."

"Sure. Talk to you later."

"SO, HOW'S YOUR DAD?"

We were eating dinner at the table when my mother popped the question. I knew it was going to come at some point, but had hoped to avoid it for a little longer.

"He's fine, Mom," I said, and smiled at Maya, who rolled her eyes at me.

Victor remained bent over his plate, eating without making any eye-contact at all or saying a word to any of us, for that matter.

"He moved here, right?" she asked, and stuck her fork in the pasta. She had hardly eaten anything except for the salad. Probably contained too many carbs for her taste. I still found it hard to accept the fact that my mother had become so fixated on looking good and eating right. It annoyed me greatly.

"Yes, he did. Right after we came here. He bought a house two blocks from here."

"I'm done," Victor said and got up from his chair. He left the kitchen without so much as looking at any of us.

My mother looked surprised. "Isn't he even supposed to take out his plate?"

"Mom," I said sounding just like Maya when she spoke to me.

"Yeah, yeah I know. Victor is special."

"He is. Things are different with him," I said, and took another plateful of the pasta. I wasn't even hungry anymore, but the stress made me continue to eat. I started wondering how many kilos I was going to gain while my mom was here. I hoped she wouldn't stay long, or else I'd have to buy new clothes.

"Seems a little like Victor is so special that he gets away with everything," she said, chirping.

I dropped my fork and looked at her. Maya got up and escaped out the door.

"Well excuse me for saying so. But he doesn't need any disciplining just because he has a *condition?*" my mother asked, making quotation signs in the air.

"Really, mom? Is that the way you're going to approach this? You've been gone for four years. What can you possibly know about my son? Do you really think I'm interested in what you think about anything?" I asked and got up from the chair. I found a bottle of red wine and opened it. I poured myself a glass.

"Oh, you're drinking too now?" my mother asked. "Is that the way you deal with everything around here? You let the boy run his own show and be so impolite that he doesn't even look at us. Meanwhile, all you do is drink and overeat. I'm really not seeing anything healthy here, Emma."

I stared at her, not believing my own ears. "What the heck do you care? You can't just run away then come back and pretend to be a mother all of a sudden, just because you don't have anything better to do."

I lifted the glass and drank some of the wine. My mother looked at me with contempt. It was hard to tell if she was upset or not, but I guessed she was. "Do you want some?" I asked, and lifted the bottle.

She nodded and looked down.

"You look like you could use it," I said, and poured her some.

I placed the glass on the table in front of her and sat down. We sat in silence for quite a while. I was furious at her and wanted to calm down before I spoke to her again. I didn't want to say something I would regret.

"I...," she said, then drank from her wine. "I missed you."

I exhaled deeply, then leaned back in my chair. "I missed you too, you old bat."

We both laughed. Then I lifted my glass and we toasted in the air. "Let's start over," I said. "Welcome back, Mom."

"Thanks, sweetie. Can't say it feels good, but I'm glad I did it, after all."

"Well you didn't have much choice, did you?"

"Ha. No, you're right. He threw me out. I don't have a penny. I've got my pension, but that's not much to live on. At least not in the lifestyle I have gotten myself used to. Damn the bastard."

I drank again. Then I looked at her. "You can stay as long as you need to," I said, knowing I was going to regret it the moment the words left my lips.

FEBRUARY 2014

Anders Samuelsen didn't like to go out. Most of the time, he stayed inside his house behind locked doors with the curtains pulled to cover the windows. He didn't care much about the world outside of his small house. He had moved outside of Nordby to be alone. He bought a house in a nice, quiet neighborhood where no one bothered each other, nor cared enough to be friendly.

It wasn't that Anders didn't like people. No, he was just so incredibly afraid of them and especially of where they had been and what they had touched. He was terrified of germs. There was nothing worse for him than that time of day when the mailman came to his door and put Anders' mail in the mailbox with his dirty germ-ridden hands and Anders had to step outside to get it. Because, not only was he afraid of germs, he was also afraid of going outside; open places especially frightened him. Anders was afraid of a lot of things and, over the years, it had come to control his life and whereabouts to a degree that his doctor told him he didn't think the medicine helped him much and that he was unable to work. The doctor had then signed a piece of paper, which he gave to the county to make them give Anders a disability pension. In that way, Anders could stay in his house and only had to go out to get the mail or that one time a week - *oh the horror* - when he had to go grocery shopping.

Anders Samuelsen liked his life the way it was and could deal with the few times when he actually had to interact with other people, even if he wanted those times to be less often. He carried with him a hand sanitizer that he used to clean his groceries before putting them in the cart and again when he came home after cleaning the door handles and washing all of his clothes.

Yes, Anders thought he had found himself safety, a way of living that he could handle. Until this morning in February when the mailman brought him a letter that, for a second, made him consider breaking out of the safety and security that he had sought for so long. A letter that made him consider leaving the house, a letter stating that *his mother had died*.

Now Anders Samuelsen wasn't particular fond of his mother. As a matter of fact, he had hated her for most of his life and some of the many therapists he'd seen blamed his condition on what had happened to him back in his childhood.

Anders had lost two younger brothers who had both died from what the doctors believed was pneumonia six months after birth. Losing two sons within three years had made Anders' mother terrified of something happening to Anders, and especially of the fact that he might also get sick. Anders' father hadn't been able to handle the big loss and had left them shortly after it. He had thereby doomed Anders to live a life where every step he took, every thing he touched was a possible danger to him. His mother preached about germs and diseases and how they travelled from person to person by air and Anders grew up to be terrified of a thing as simple as breathing.

At the age of seventeen, Anders had run away from home, only to find himself living on the street and soon being hospitalized with pneumonia. His mother had come to his bed and told him he was a fool and he had brought this on himself, and when he had asked her to let him live his life like a normal teenager, she told him that if that was what he wanted, then she was done trying to take care of him. She had left him in the hospital with a check on the table and told him to go out and take care of himself. She was done. If he wanted to get sick, then she wasn't going to stand by and watch it.

"It's like a Band-Aid," she said. "Hurts less if you rip it off fast."

And then she was gone.

Now Anders sat in his small house that he had bought with the money his mother had given him and looked at the letter from the attorney stating that she had died from falling from a ladder, while disinfecting the kitchen cabinets. Anders chuckled.

Of course she would go out cleaning.

But it wasn't the fact that she died or how she went that had gotten Anders thinking about leaving his house for this news. No, it was the fact that his mother was an extremely wealthy woman and the attorney stated in the letter that Anders had to contact him, so they could discuss his inheritance.

You could get a bigger house. Pay someone to do the grocery-shopping for you. Make sure you never had to go outside again.

The thought made Anders smile for the first time in many months. He got up from the chair and found his phone in the drawer. Wearing plastic gloves, he dialed the attorney's number.

9

FEBRUARY 2014

I was exhausted when I woke up the next morning. I had slept horribly, constantly tossing and turning and worrying about this whole thing with my mother and whether it was a mistake to tell her she could stay as long as she needed to.

But she was, after all, my mother. Wasn't I obligated to help her out? I knew she wasn't here because she wanted to suddenly be close to all of us again. No, she was here because she had nowhere else to go. That's what bothered me so much.

At the same time, I was afraid of hurting my dad. I would have to tell him at some point that she was back and that she had moved in. I felt bad for him, since this was not at all what he needed right now. He had finally moved on and put their marriage behind him. I had no idea how he was going to react to this.

Why now? Of all the times you could chose to interfere in my life, dear mother, why now? You really know how to time things.

Furthermore, I was very concerned about that strange message carved in the skin of the dead woman. It freaked me out. I had no idea what this killer wanted from me or why he would choose to carve a message to me on the back of a dead woman. Did he want to tell me something? Who did the body belong to? And worst of all; would there be any more?

I had the chills thinking about it when I went downstairs to start making breakfast for my kids before school. I opened the door to the kitchen and, to my great surprise, found my mother standing there, wearing an apron.

"You're up early," I said, and stepped inside. I noticed, to my pleasure, that there was coffee in the pot and I poured myself a cup. I closed my eyes and sipped it, then spat it all out in the sink.

"What the...? What is that?"

"Ganoderma coffee. I brought a package with me from Spain," my mother sang happily. Her cheerfulness annoyed me.

"That tastes horrible, Mom."

"It's better for you. Ganoderma coffee is like regular coffee but contains extracts of Ganoderma. It's a medical mushroom, in case you didn't know."

"A mushroom? Come on, Mom. I really like my own coffee. Regular black coffee with milk. Nothing else."

"Ganoderma on its own offers certain health benefits. Aren't you even interested in that?"

"Not really."

"Oh come on, sweetheart. There is so much to learn. For instance: a study of some advanced-stage cancer patients found that Ganoderma strengthened the immune system in people with cancer. Published in *Immunological Investigations*, the study found that 12 weeks of treatment with Ganoderma supplements enhanced immune response in most participants. They say it can knock out breast cancer cells and lower cholesterol."

"But I don't have breast cancer, at least not that I know of, and I don't have a high cholesterol level either. If I ever get any of those two, I'll get back to you and have you make me some of that coffee."

My mother scoffed. "Don't be such a dinosaur, Emma. Try something new for once. It's not just those things it's good for. It's also a strong antioxidant. It can boost your immunity, help with weight loss, fight fatigue and improve memory, relieve stress and reverse the aging process. Who doesn't want that, huh?"

"Me," I said, and poured the rest of the cup into the sink. "I don't need all of that. My immune system is great. I haven't been sick since we moved here. I have no stress and my memory works just fine, sometimes a little too great, if you ask me. It would be nice to forget stuff every now and then, especially when you want to sleep, if you know what I mean. And I look just fine. I don't care about aging or weight loss. There, now I'll make a new fresh pot of my own coffee, if you don't mind."

"Well, you should," my mother snorted, just as Maya and Victor came through the door.

"Should what?" Maya asked and sat down.

My mother smiled at her. "Look at how beautiful she is. Look at that skin. It's perfect."

Maya made a grimace.

"Don't do that, Maya," my mother corrected her. "Don't frown like that. It'll give you wrinkles."

Are you kidding me, Mom? Talking about wrinkles to a four-teen-year-old? Don't you think her self-esteem has it hard enough being a teenager and all?

"Mom should what?" Maya asked again.

"Your grandmother thinks I'm getting fat and old and she thinks I should be more concerned with that, which I'm not, since I don't care about those things. I think there are many other things more valuable to focus on in life."

I poured Victor a bowl of cereal, like usual, when my mother stopped me.

"I baked," she said, and opened the oven. "Gluten-free, no wheat," she said with a smile.

I frowned. "Mom, we're really not into all that stuff. We like real food."

"Just try it," she said, and pulled the bread out. She cut a slice and put it on a plate. "Here, give the boy that instead of that sugary stuff in the cereal box."

"Mom, Victor always gets his cereal. This is the way he likes it and that's what he is getting."

"I'd like some," Maya said, and raised her hand.

"Nice to know that there is at least someone sensible here in the house," my mother said and cut her a piece. "Cheese on it?"

"Sure," Maya said.

"Here you go my dear."

Maya took a bite, then smiled. "This is actually not so bad, Mom. You should try it."

I bit my lip and growled, then placed the bowl of cereal in front of Victor, who started eating immediately.

"Don't be late for school," I said, when my phone suddenly rang.

It was Morten.

"Just wanted to say good morning," he said.

"Well, good morning to you as well," I answered and left the kitchen to be able to talk more privately. "How'd it go yesterday? With the mother of the deceased woman? How'd she take it?"

Morten exhaled. "It wasn't good. I'll tell you that much. She was very upset."

"Well that's natural. Could she tell you anything useful?" I asked.

"Only that she had suspected for a couple of days that Susie hadn't taken her medicine. She had been trying to hide it, but the mother sensed that she might have been manic in the days before her death. You know how people with bipolar disorder have either manic days or depressive days."

"Yeah, like there is nothing in between. They never have just ordinary days unless they're on medicine."

"Susie often cheated on her meds, her mother told me. She had gotten good at hiding it from her mother, but there was something in her behavior lately that tipped her off. She was actually going to ask her about it on the day she disappeared. Anyway, I have no idea if it means anything, but it was worth writing down."

"Sure. Any news on the body and who it belongs to?"

"I'm on my way down to the station right now. We're waiting for the forensics team to ID her. I hope it'll be later today."

"Then off to tell yet another relative the bad news, huh?"

"Yes, I know. I just want to get it over with."

"Did you search Susie's home?"

"We did. We didn't find much, though. Nothing that could connect her with you. She didn't even have any of your books. But the strangest thing was, we didn't find any of her meds. Her mother said she had several kinds of medicine that she took and that they usually were in the cabinet in the bathroom. But we never found any of them."

"That's odd," I said pensively.

"That's what I thought. Anyway how are things with you? Getting any writing done?" he asked.

"Well, no. I'm kind of stuck on that. Furthermore, I have a visitor. An unexpected one who's a little annoying. One of those you can't say no to, but really wish would leave soon."

"Oh oh. That doesn't sound good. A family member?"

"My mother."

"Ah, I see. Well how bad can it be?"

"It's horrible. You have no idea."

"Why is it so bad?"

"Where to start? First of all, she left all of us four years ago without any explanation. She hurt both me and my dad and it's a little hard to accept the fact that she all of a sudden wants back in our lives. I have no idea how my dad is going to react. Second of all, she's on this freaking health trip and now she wants all of us to join in. She has seriously baked a gluten-free, wheat-free bread. I mean, what is even in that? What is it with people and gluten these days? Does anyone even know what it is and why we all of a sudden can't eat it?"

Morten burst into laughter. "Oh I needed that," he said. "A good laugh. Well, I guess you have your hands full. Is it really that bad?"

"It is. Now she is having Maya eat it."

"So she baked a bread. What is so bad about that?" Morten asked.

"You're missing the point. It isn't the fact that she baked bread that annoys me. I love baking myself and love it when someone else bakes for me. No, it's the fact that she's come here with all her wrong values about how appearance is the most important thing, and now she is putting them all on my daughter. I don't like it. I really don't."

Morten chuckled. "I think you might be putting a little too much into a loaf of bread."

"Really? You should hear her. All she talks about is how she thinks I'm getting old and fat and that I eat all wrong and...and you should see her, Morten. She's had so many facelifts, I swear she looks almost Asian. She is pumped with Botox, how is that for healthy living, huh? To pump your face with toxins."

Just as I said the last words, I turned and spotted my mother who was standing right behind me. My heart dropped.

"Well maybe she's just very insecure," Morten said on the other end.

I stared at my mother, not knowing what to say. "I gotta go."

I hung up.

"Mom...I...I'm s..."

"I just wanted to tell you that I made you another pot of coffee. Your usual kind and not the kind that is spiked with wrong values."

Then she turned around and went back into the kitchen.

Me and my awfully big mouth.

10

MARCH 2002

L*iving in fear is the norm in my house*, Alexandra thought to herself while watching her now six-year-old son Samuel play with his cars outside on the tiles on their patio. He was making the cars bang into each other violently and then he'd throw them through the air against the window where Alexandra was standing.

I should say something. I shouldn't let him get away with that. I shouldn't let him just throw the cars at the window. It might break. I should tell him that. Tell him to stop, that it is wrong behavior. I really should.

But Alexandra realized she didn't dare. She couldn't risk him throwing another of his fits. Last time she told him to clean up his clothes after himself when he had thrown them on the floor in the hallway, he spat at her, ran into the kitchen, and broke every glass and plate he could find. She'd hid in her bedroom with her heart hammering in her chest until he went quiet, hours later. When she came down, the boy had not only broken everything he could get his hands on, he had also smeared feces all over the walls.

That was when Alexandra finally sought help. She took the boy to specialists on the mainland for an evaluation. The first evaluation brought a diagnosis of Sensory Integration Disorder. They told her Samuel simply couldn't live in his body. His levels of hyperactivity, impulsiveness, and aggression were off the charts. More evaluations and consultations by top professionals revealed severe ADHD and an unspecified Mood Disorder. Alexandra read every book she could find on ADHD and the other diagnoses. She tried different behavioral plans, special diets, therapies, and all other approaches she could find.

Nothing worked.

Alexandra thought about all the hours she had put into finding out what was wrong with the boy and shook her head in despair. It was wearing on them, tearing their marriage apart. Poul was almost never home anymore and often he isolated himself in the garage where he was fixing up an old car. He never spoke much to the boy, which seemed to only worsen his condition. Caring for Samuel seemed to be all that Alexandra's life was about and it was exhausting her. She had no energy for her husband and they were drifting apart rapidly. Her life had been reduced to being about nothing more than getting by day-by-day, hour-by-hour.

Samuel was in school now and, in the beginning, that had helped slightly with the situation. Every now and then, he could be the old caring and loving Samuel that Alexandra remembered him to be and, on those days, she was determined to never give up on him. But on the bad days, he seemed to be preoccupied with aggressive and violent thoughts, telling her that *bad things came into his head*...Telling her he loved weapons and dreamed about killing. Those were the days when she wondered if it was even worth it to keep trying. She never knew what mood he'd come home in and, even if it was good, it could shift in an instant. He could snap and, suddenly, everything changed. She would be afraid of him and fear what he might do to her.

It was the most terrifying feeling in the world. To be afraid of your own child.

Luckily, this day had been good so far. Samuel had come home from school telling her he had fun, then run outside to play. It had been at least two months since his last serious tantrum so maybe, just maybe things were shaping up a little? Maybe he was, after all, getting better?

His last one had been bad, though. It had happened in class when another student had taken Samuel's crayons and cracked all of them. Then Samuel had taken a pair of scissors and stabbed the classmate in the arm. The scissors had gone through the skin and the boy had been in the hospital when the principal had called in Alexandra and Poul for a talk about Samuel's *future* at the school. Alexandra told his story and, considering his condition, they didn't expel him...not yet at least. Alexandra dreaded the day when they would. And it would come. She was certain it would.

Alexandra stared at her boy, enjoying the peace in the house while he was playing outside. Her phone rang and she went into the kitchen to pick it up. It was her mother who had called for no apparent reason. Alexandra talked to her for a few minutes, then returned to check on her son. Samuel was still sitting on the tiles, but the character of his play had changed drastically. He was no longer playing with his cars. He had caught a black bird that he was now torturing by cutting off its wings and legs with a small kitchen knife.

Alexandra gasped and knocked on the window.

"Stop that, Samuel. Stop that immediately!" she yelled. "Leave the poor bird alone. Do you hear me? Samuel!"

Samuel turned his head like an owl and stared directly at her. He held the bloody knife up in the air.

"I heard you Mommy, dear. I heard you loud and clear."

Then he laughed.

11

FEBRUARY 2014

"**M**om, I..."
I stepped inside the kitchen and found her standing by the counter, staring out the window. Maya yelled that she and Victor were leaving for school.

"Bye, sweetheart," I yelled back, wishing myself back to the days when she would kiss me endlessly before leaving and didn't want to let go of me in the mornings because she hated to leave me alone.

"It's okay, Emma," my mom said, and wrapped her bread in foil. "Just know that I'm trying here, alright?"

I grabbed the coffeepot and poured myself a cup. It smelled heavenly. "I know you are," I said. "It's just..."

She turned to look at me. I hated the fact that she looked the same no matter what mood she was in. Her eyes told me she was upset.

"It's just what?" she asked.

"It's just all a little overwhelming right now. I mean, you haven't been a part of my...of *our* lives for four years now and, all of a sudden, you come back and expect us to just forget everything?"

My mom exhaled. I sipped my coffee, thinking I really needed the caffeine right now.

"I know," she said. "It was silly of me to think that there was still a place for me here, that my family actually had missed me."

"We did. I did a lot. But it's gonna take some time to get used to...and especially with all the new stuff. All the health stuff. It's not...It's not how I remember you."

My mother looked confused. She wanted to say something, but was interrupted when someone rang the doorbell. I put the cup down and went to open it. Outside in the snow stood the mailman. He was smiling.

"I have a package for you today, Emma. It looks big."

He held it up. It was big alright. Then he put it on the ground and handed me the clipboard.

"You just need to sign here."

I grabbed the clipboard and pen and signed it. The mailman kept smiling and looking at the package.

"Sure is a big one. What is it?"

I shrugged. "I have no idea. I didn't order anything, as far as I know. Maybe it's for Maya. She always orders all kinds of stuff. Come to think of it, she did order some clothes. That's probably it."

"Hope she didn't max out your credit card on this one," the mailman said.

I smiled and shook my head. "Me too."

I grabbed the package and lifted it in the air. "Well I'd better get it inside. Thanks."

The mailman lifted his cap and nodded. "My pleasure."

I went back inside to my mother in the kitchen and placed the package on the kitchen table.

"What on earth is that?" she asked.

"I have no idea. There is no sender on it. It might be something Maya ordered."

"But it has your name on it?"

"That is strange. Maybe it is for me after all?" I said. "I'm opening it to see what it is."

"I'll get the scissors," my mother said, and handed them to me.

I cut off the tape, then ripped the package open. It was filled with bubble wrap. I pulled it out and threw it on the table. Then I saw something.

"What is it?" my mother asked.

"I don't know. It looks strange..."

I reached my hand down and grabbed whatever it was between my hands, then pulled it up.

"Oh my God," my mother gasped.

I looked down and, as I realized what it was that I was holding, I immediately dropped it and started to scream.

12

FEBRUARY 2014

"**W**HAT THE HELL IS THAT?!" My mother couldn't stop screaming. She clapped her hands to her mouth. I looked at her, then down at the head that had landed back in the box when I dropped it. Its bloody eyes looked back at me. My heart was pounding rapidly. I stumbled backwards. I touched my face in frustration, then realized they were smeared in blood from holding the head.

"What was it, Emma?" My mother continued. "It...it...it looked like...Tell me it wasn't, Emma. Tell me it wasn't."

"I...I'm afraid it was..."

"Where did it come from? Emma? What is going on here? Talk to me. Why was there a head in that box?"

"I don't know, for crying out loud. I don't know, Mom!"

My entire body was shivering as I kept walking backwards, away from the staring head in the box, so it wouldn't be able to look at me anymore.

I heard a noise at the front door. Someone was knocking, then the door opened. "Hello? Is everyone alright in here? I heard screaming."

The door to the kitchen opened slowly and the mailman peeked in. He looked at my mother, then at me. "What happened?" he asked, horrified.

"The box you handed me," I said. "It...it..."

"There was a head in it," my mother said from behind her hands.

The mailman looked at her, then walked towards her and looked inside the box. "Oh my God," he exclaimed, then closed the lid. He looked at my mother again. "Are you alright?"

She removed her hands from her mouth, then shook her head. "Who...who would do such a thing?"

The mailman put a hand on her shoulder. "You look pale, Mrs. Don't you want to sit down?"

He pulled out a chair and helped my mom sit. "Miss," she said. "I'm divorced."

The mailman lit up. "Oh, well, then miss...?"

"Ulla," my mother said. "You can call me Ulla."

"Very well. Would you care for a glass of water, Ulla?"

"Yes, please. That would be nice."

The mailman found a glass and poured tap water into it, then handed it to my mom. I heard the front door open and more people enter. Seconds later, Sophia opened the door to the kitchen with a loud bang.

"What's going on here?" She looked at the mailman and my mother, who both looked like schoolchildren caught kissing in the schoolyard.

Sophia turned and saw me. "Are you alright?" she asked.

I looked at her, then shook my head. I pointed at the box on the wooden kitchen table.

"You don't want to look in there," the mailman said.

"I'll decide that for myself," Sophia said, and opened the box. She blinked a couple of times, then closed the lid again. "Well, that explains a lot."

I turned on the water and started washing my hands, frantically scrubbing them to get the blood off. Then I found my cellphone and called Morten.

"You need to come immediately," I said. "Someone sent me a woman's head in the mail."

Morten arrived with blaring sirens, then stormed inside, looking at me. I was still standing by the sink rubbing my hands with a towel, trying to remove the feeling of having someone else's blood on me.

"Are you okay?" he asked.

"Yes. Just take that thing away from me," I said.

My mother gasped as Morten opened the lid and looked inside. The mailman took her hand in his and put the other on her shoulder.

Sophia opened a bottle of whiskey and poured some in a glass that she handed to me. "Here, this should calm you down."

I had never been much of a drinker during the daytime, but this day I really did need something strong. I took it with shivering hands, then gulped it down.

"Thanks. That helped."

Sophia smiled. "One more?"

I shook my head. "No thanks."

She poured herself one and pounded it down while Morten studied the head in the box, while wearing plastic gloves. "I need to take this to the forensics team," he said. "I have a feeling I know who it belongs to."

He looked at me and I nodded. I thought about the decapitated woman's body I'd seen the day before and felt nauseated. "Just take it out of here, please," I said again.

"Why would anyone send this to Emma?" my mother asked.

Morten shrugged. "That's what I hope we can figure out." He looked down in the box again as he was closing the lid, then stopped. He opened it again, then stuck his hand inside and pulled out an envelope in a small plastic bag. It was smeared in blood.

"What's this?" he asked.

I shrugged and moved forward. "I haven't seen it until now."

He looked at it, then back at me. "It's addressed to you."

My heart started pounding in my chest again. I walked towards him, then pulled it out of his hands.

"At least wear some gloves, so we won't ruin possible finger-prints," he said and handed me a fresh pair of gloves.

I put them on, then opened the plastic bag and pulled out the white envelope with my name on it. I started tearing it open while trying to calm my heart down. All eyes in the room were on me as I pulled out a letter.

"What does it say?" my mother asked.

I opened the letter and read it. Then I scoffed. "What the hell is this supposed to mean?" I asked and looked at Morten.

I showed him the letter. He read it out loud:

"*Tag...you're it?*" He looked at me again. "What the heck does that mean?"

"You tell me. The first message was *Peek-a-boo.*"

"Both are kids' games. Someone is playing games with you, Emma?" Sophia asked.

"Looks like it," Morten said.

"Looks more like a bad joke, if you ask me," I said, and took off my gloves.

"What is going on here, officer?" my mom asked with shivering voice. "Is Emma in danger?"

"We don't know yet, Mrs. Frost," Morten said.

"It's Miss Lisholm," she corrected him. "I went back to my maiden name after the divorce."

"Sorry about that, Miss Lisholm," Morten said. He took the letter and put it back in the bag. "I'll have to take this as well."

"Take everything," I said. "Get it out of here."

"I'll have the forensic team look at it, then get back to you with the results. In the meantime, I encourage you to not be alone."

"There aren't many chances I will," I said, and looked at my mother who was still holding the mailman's hand, much to my surprise.

Morten took the box, then forced a smile. "I'll call you later, okay?"

"Okay."

When he was gone, everyone in the room looked at me.

"What?" I asked.

"What do you think this is all about?" my mother asked. "I'm really worried about you. What is going on here?"

I shrugged. "I don't know. Some idiot finds it funny to leave me creepy messages along with dead bodies." I paused.

My mother's eyes looked appalled.

"What do you want me to say?" I asked.

"Well, I'd better be going now," the mailman said, and finally let go of my mother's hand. "People are waiting for their mail."

"Thank you so much for all your help, Mr....?" My mother said.

"Arne," the mailman replied. "Just call me Arne."

"Well thank you, Arne," my mother chirped, as she walked him out. "Thank you for being such a gentleman. There aren't many of those left these days."

13

FEBRUARY 2014

There was only one thing Anders Samuelsen hated more than open spaces and that was small closed rooms. Ever since he was a teenager, he had suffered from a severe claustrophobia, one that prevented him from taking any elevator, train, bus or plane. The thought of being cramped together with hundreds of people without being able to get away when you wanted to, was simply petrifying to him.

So naturally, Anders reacted with fear right away when he opened his eyes and found himself in complete darkness. It seemed to be a small room, with walls so close he could reach out and touch them on both sides of where he was lying. Panic spread when he touched the walls surrounding him, feeling the wood to sense if it was movable, pressing on it to see if he could push it aside, but he couldn't. Above him, he could touch what appeared to be the roof of the dark room he was in. His body seemed to be lying on something soft. It felt like silk.

What was this place? He could barely move. He couldn't see.

"Help!" Anders yelled. "Help me? Someone? I can't see anything. Please turn on the light. Someone. Anyone?"

A light was turned on. Anders gasped and looked up to spot a small lamp in the corner. It was so strong, it almost blinded him when he looked at it. He turned his head with a moan and tried to look around. Then his heart stopped. The room he was in was even smaller than he thought. As a matter of fact, it wasn't a room at all. He was in a box of some sort. All the walls were black and he couldn't see what was on the other side. Anders screamed, then looked up at the small lamp in the corner. There was something else next to it. What was that? It looked like...like a small camera?

Oh my God, oh dear God. Where am I? Please get me out of here. I promise I'll be good. I promise. Please!

Anders looked into the camera hoping there would be someone looking from the other end of it.

"Please," he pleaded. "Please get me out of here. I hate small spaces. I really, really hate small spaces. Please help me."

Anders fought his tears, but knew he wouldn't be able to hold them back much longer. He lifted his leg and started kicking the roof, then the sides of the box, but nothing helped. It didn't move.

"HEEEEELP!" he screamed, while kicking and crying. The feeling of utter panic spread slowly, like a cancer through his body and filled him with despair, causing him to kick and hit the sides of the box even more frantically.

Why is this happening to me, God? Why me? Please. I'm so scared. I have to get out. I have to...simply have to get out!

But none of the kicking and banging on the sides, nor on the roof or the floor of the box helped. It didn't move an inch. Not an opening in sight.

How the hell did I even end up in here?

He tried to remember what had happened. The letter! He had received the letter telling him his mother had died.

Did she do this to me?

No, the thought was absurd. She was dead, for crying out loud. Anders shook his head, trying to remember. He had taken a chance.

Oh, why did you do that? You knew it would end badly. You

knew going outside would be a terrible mistake. You did it anyway, you fool! Look at what happened!

He had called for a taxi to go to the lawyer's office. That's right. He had called for a taxi. It had arrived at his house and he had gotten in and told the driver the address. The driver had smiled in the rearview mirror, then said the words.

"As you wish, sir."

Then he had driven off. What had happened next? It was so hard for Anders to remember. He remembered driving through town, he also remembered going past the address that he had given the driver. Then he remember telling the driver to stop, that he had passed the address, that he had to go back, but the driver hadn't said anything. Instead, he had sped the car up. Anders felt scared, but tried to talk to him again, when suddenly the driver had stepped on the brakes. Anders remembered screaming as the car came to a very sudden stop, the tires screeching. He remembered yelling at the driver, telling him he was a horrible driver, then grabbing the door handle with his gloved hands to try and open the door, but not being able to. He had known something was really wrong, but didn't want to believe it. He had told the driver to open up, but the driver had laughed at him, then turned around and faced him. Thinking back on it, Anders shivered at the look he remembered on his face. It wasn't the coldness in his eyes or the manic smile on his face that scared him. No, it was the fact that the driver had sneezed at that very moment, spreading all of his germs in the car and Anders knew, he just knew in his scared mind, that there was no way he could avoid those small airborne bastards. He couldn't stop them from entering his fragile body. Even if he covered his mouth and nose, they would find their way through the tear-ducts in his eyes. He knew that much from the many books he had read and TV shows he had seen on the subject, describing it in the smallest detail, with graphics. The driver had laughed again, then lifted his hand which was holding something, what was it? Oh yes, a small spray can of some sort. Terrified, Anders had seen him press it and spray something into Anders' face and, soon after, he remembered nothing except for the strong smell and the taste of ether in his mouth.

Anders drew in a deep breath, thinking this wasn't an accident. He had been sedated, then placed here in this box by this germ-spreading driver-person. But why? Why would he do this to him?

Then a thought struck him. What if someone had put him inside of this box to kill him? To finish him off? Panicking again, he stared at the box, at the corners, and sides to look for just a small opening, anything where air could come in, but he found none. He gasped for air. He could already sense how it was getting harder for him to breathe. How his throat constricted.

Calm down Anders. You have to save your air until help arrives. You have to stay calm.

Crying and sobbing, he looked up at the camera again.

"Please. Please HELP ME!"

14

FEBRUARY 2014

"I guess it's no surprise," Morten said on the phone, "but the head sent to you *is* the one that belongs to the body we found outside of City Hall yesterday."

"Well at least no more have been killed then," I said.

It was afternoon when Morten called and I was waiting for Maya and Victor to come home from school. I had baked some of my very unhealthy wheat gluten-packed buns and had sent my mom into the living room, where she was sitting with her laptop checking her e-mail and Facebook.

Meanwhile, Sophia had taken off for work, even though she had insisted on staying for a while to be there for me. Alma had started daycare and Sophia was back in her part-time teaching job at the local school, which she loved.

Finally, I had some time to myself before the kids came back and I enjoyed it immensely. I was still shaken by this morning's events, but I tried to not let it get to me. I couldn't shake the feeling that the two women had died because of me, somehow, and that made me feel terrible.

"Are you alright?" Morten asked on the phone.

"I will be," I said. "Did you ID the second woman?"

"As a matter of fact, we did. It wasn't too hard once we had the head...," he cleared his throat. "I mean, since it's a small island and everything. So when I brought it down to the station, my colleague Allan immediately recognized her."

"So, who was she?"

"Tine Solvang. She was a social worker down at City Hall," he said. "Went missing after a fight with her husband a year ago. Hasn't been seen since. Everyone thought she had left the island and gone back to Copenhagen where she originally came from... even her husband, since he received a letter from her telling him that she had left him and that she never wanted to see him again. It was sent from Copenhagen."

"Wow," I said. "A year ago, you say?"

"Yes. The forensics people told me her body had been frozen. It's hard to determine the exact time of death, but they believe she was killed about twelve months ago, then frozen until a couple of days ago when her body was thawed and the head cut off. It was definitely done after she was killed and the body frozen."

"How was she killed? There was blood on her face," I said, remembering how I had gotten it on my fingers and scrubbed them to get it off.

"That's another story." Morten exhaled. This was tough, even on him, I could hear. "The blood on her face wasn't Tine's."

"Then whose was it? Susie Larsen's?"

"Apparently not."

"So maybe it was his?" I asked hopefully.

"That's what we hope. But there's another possibility. One I don't like to think of."

I covered my mouth with my hand. "It might be from another victim?"

"Well, we don't know yet. We're getting it analyzed in the lab."

I grabbed a chair and sat down, touching my forehead in distress.

"So, he's planned this for a long time, huh?" I asked.

"At least a year, maybe even more," Morten said with a heavy voice.

"And what part do I play in it all?"

"That's what we need to find out."

"Please, do it quickly," I said and spotted Victor and Maya walking past the kitchen window. "I don't want any more people to die because of me."

"Emma, you need to let go of that thought. If he hadn't chosen you to deliver his message to, he would have chosen someone else. It's not your fault. You hear me?"

The front door opened and I could hear my children in the hallway, taking off their winter boots and heavy jackets.

"Whatever," I said. "Just catch this guy for me, will you? Please?"

Morten chuckled. "Anything for you. You know that."

I smiled and waved at Maya as she entered the kitchen, looking cold with her rosy cheeks and red nose tip. "I know. Gotta go."

"Talk to you later."

15

FEBRUARY 2014

"**H**OW WAS YOUR DAY, SWEETHEART?**"
Maya exhaled and sat down in a chair. "The usual,"
she said.

"And you Victor? Did you have a good day?"

"Why?"

I smiled. "I know I ask the same question every day. But did anything exciting happen today?"

"No."

I felt the buns to see if they were cool enough to eat, then picked a couple and put them in a basket that I placed at the table. "Did you learn anything new?" I asked Victor. He wasn't looking at me, but for once, I seemed to have his attention and I wasn't going to let it go easily.

"No."

I buttered a bun and placed it in front of him. He started eating, still staring down at the table.

"What's your subject in History?"

I only asked because I knew Victor loved history lessons and he could spend hours in his room reading about the French revolution, which was his favorite subject.

"The Battle of Copenhagen on April 2nd, 1801."

I buttered a bun for myself and started eating as well. Maya only had a glass of juice.

"You're not having any?" I said, a little hurt.

"I'm not that hungry. Plus, I don't think all this gluten is good for you. I prefer Grandma's bread."

I scoffed, knowing she only said it to hurt me, which she succeeded at, but I pretended she didn't. "Well, suit yourself. You're missing out, right Victor?"

"I'm done," he said and got up. "I'm going to play in the yard."

"Don't forget to get your snowsuit on. And gloves," I yelled after him, but he was already gone.

"I should be going too," Maya said and got up.

"Where are you going?"

"I have homework, then I promised Grandma I'd take her downtown to visit the organic health store."

"The organic health store, huh?" I sipped my coffee and bit down on my buttered bun. "Well, have fun. Go crazy."

"Thanks, Mom," Maya said, and stormed out of the kitchen.

I exhaled and leaned back, not knowing what to think of it all. At least Maya wasn't doing drugs or hanging out with boys at the harbor. But a health freak? My daughter? I couldn't believe it. I grabbed my laptop from the table and opened it. While finishing my bun, I opened my mailbox and scrolled through my e-mails. I sipped my coffee, while going through all the e-mails from my readers telling me how much they loved my books, asking for signed copies, and so on. I answered as many as I could, then opened a new e-mail. It seemed to be from another fan, but as soon as I read further down, I realized it wasn't. As I read the letter, my heart started pounding. Then I grabbed the phone.

"Morten, I think I've received an e-mail from the killer."

"What are you saying?" he asked, startled.

"I've received a very strange e-mail. I think it might be from the killer of those women."

"What does it say? Can you read it to me?"

"It all seems a little strange. It starts with *Dear Emma Frost. I'm a great fan of your work.* Then it gets weirder. *I'm sorry to have been so drastic in my way of getting your attention, but it is hard these days to be noticed. Now that I have your full attention, we can move on. Do you like to play, Emma Frost? I do. My favorite game as a child used to be Hide and Go Seek. Do you want to play Hide and Go Seek with me, Emma Frost? I think you do. Here's the deal. Attached to this e-mail you'll find a video and some information. If you know how to connect the dots correctly, you'll win. Isn't this fun? But you must hurry, Emma. As you watch the video, you'll understand. Time is of the essence here. Good luck. It's already so much fun playing with you. Yours sincerely.*"

"Then what does it say?" Morten asked. "Is there a name? Anything?"

"No, there's nothing. No name, nothing. Not even a sender on the e-mail. I can't reply to it."

"That's the oddest thing I've heard in a long time," Morten said, puzzled. "Have you looked at the attachments?"

"No. I'm pressing play on the video now," I said, and moved the cursor.

A picture of a guy showed up on my screen. He was panting and desperately knocking on the walls of, what appeared to be, a small box that he was in. He was crying and screaming desperately, pleading into the camera for help.

I gasped.

"What is it?" Morten asked.

"I think you better come over here."

16

FEBRUARY 2014

"**W**HAT'S GOING ON?**"**
Morten stormed into the kitchen a few minutes
after we'd hung up. I was still looking at the screen on my
computer, trying hard to calm myself and my desperately beating
heart down.

"I...it's...It looks like a guy is trapped in a box somewhere," I said.
"Why? Why would anyone send a video like this?"

"Let me see," Morten said.

I pulled away so he could better see. "Please tell me what the
heck is going on here, Morten. Who is doing these things? The two
women, the head in the box and now this? Tell me you have a
suspect. Something."

Morten exhaled, tired. "I'm sorry. We don't have anything yet."
He looked at the screen where the man was knocking on the roof of
the box while screaming for help.

"Who is he?" I asked.

"I don't know. This is awful. We can't even tell if the guy is alive
or if the video is old."

"It's a live feed," I said.

Morten looked at me. "It's happening right now?"

"Yes. That man is in that box right now. And see the clock in the corner?"

"It's counting down?"

"My guess is that is how long the guy has left before he runs out of air," I said. "The killer attached some documents from NASA as well as some about how much Oxygen a person needs at rest in an airtight space. At first I didn't understand them, but then I saw the small clock in the corner of the live stream and then I understood."

"So he has less than two hours left?" Morten asked.

"Guess so."

Morten pulled his hair. "And we have no idea what the killer wants, do we?"

"None whatsoever. There are no demands in this e-mail and, as I said, I can't even reply to it to ask what it is he wants."

"Have you looked through all of the attachments?" Morten asked.

"I have. But it makes no sense. It's mostly newspaper clippings about a place on the island that is about to close, then there are statistics about young people with psychiatric diseases...I...I really don't get it."

"Let me have a look at it," Morten said, and opened the attachments. He looked at the numbers and scrolled through the reports.

"It's a lot, right? I mean, we can't sit here and read all this while the guy is running out of air. We need to do something."

"But the answer has to be in these documents, somehow," Morten said. "Wasn't that what the letter said? You had to connect the dots to win?"

"Yes, but...What if he is just a maniac and none of it makes any sense? Then we're going to be too late," I said. "The poor guy will die."

"What is this place that the articles are talking about?" Morten asked, and started reading.

"It's this place called Hummelgaarden. It's an institution for young kids with psychiatric problems," I said.

"And it's closing? Why?"

"Apparently, because the city can't afford to run it, but some of the articles say it's because the neighbors don't want it. They say it devalues their houses and make them afraid in case one of the youngsters runs loose and attacks one of the neighbors or their children. But, officially, it's because there's no money." I paused and looked at Morten. "I think you're right."

"What are you saying?"

"Maybe the killer wants something after all," I said.

"Like what?"

"He wants us to stop the closing of Hummelgaarden. Don't you see? All these statistics show how many young people with mental diseases there are who commit crimes...and then this place that tries to help them is being closed. I think he wants us to save the place."

"A killer with a noble motive? It sounds a little out there."

"I know. It does. I mean, he killed two women to get our attention about this, why would he do such a thing? Unless..."

"Unless there was a message in it," Morten said. "One was a social worker, the other a young woman who was diagnosed with bipolar disorder when she was in her teens."

"Of course," I exclaimed. "That's why he put the head of the patient on the body of a social worker. It was all part of the message."

"Because it's in the head she was sick and needed help."

"Just like the kids placed in Hummelgaarden."

Morten sighed and leaned back in his chair. "Wow that's a lot to take in at once. So how do we do it? How do we save this guy?"

"We raise enough money to keep Hummelgaarden open."

17

MAY 2006

"I love you so much mom!"

"I love you too, Samuel," Alexandra said, forcing a smile.

You don't mean that. Why are you lying to the boy? The fact is, you can't stand him. You're scared to death of him, even on the good days.

She was standing in the kitchen cutting carrots for dinner when Samuel came up to her and said the words. She looked at him only briefly, afraid to say or do something that might cause another of his fits. The fact was, he could be so sweet and loving at one moment, but then change in an instant and Alexandra was never prepared for when that was.

Unlike Poul who had stopped talking to the boy at all, Alexandra hadn't given up on Samuel yet. She still believed that somewhere, deep inside, the real Samuel was hiding and that there was a way to help him. But, as she had experienced in the last several years, there wasn't much help to get anywhere.

Samuel is a troublemaker, the school said, when they expelled him.

He needs better discipline, the social worker said, when Alexandra tried to get help from the county.

He has a bad temper, he'll grow out of it, the doctor said.

Meanwhile, Alexandra had to deal with the boy every day now, since no school on the island would take him. She had to quit her own job to homeschool him and she had no idea how to do it.

"What's for dinner?" Samuel asked, still smiling.

Alexandra's hands were shaking as she whispered the answer. "Meatballs and potatoes."

She closed her eyes, waiting for the boy's response. He usually liked meatballs, but like so many other things, that could change. He could suddenly decide he hated meatballs and start throwing things.

She never knew.

"I love meatballs," he said.

Alexandra sighed, relieved, and opened her eyes. Samuel looked at her and smiled. She felt fear rise inside of her, knowing how easily that smile and those eyes could suddenly turn pitch-black, and she would see nothing but evil on his face.

"That's good then," she said, and returned to chopping the carrots. She didn't like the way the boy stared at the knife, which made her hold it more tightly in her hand.

What am I to do with you, my boy? How can this ever end happily?

She had tried everything and everybody. She had sought out all the experts, even tried to medicate the boy, but nothing helped. No one understood her. No one understood how she could be afraid of her own son, of a ten-year-old boy. But she was. She was terrified of him. Every day she woke up, she feared what the day with him would bring. Homeschooling him was close to impossible and she had almost given up. Poul had suggested they send the boy away, to a boarding school on the mainland and Alexandra was tempted, but still didn't like the idea of giving up on the boy.

"When is dinner going to be ready, Mom?" Samuel asked.

Alexandra swallowed hard. "Half an hour."

"But I'm hungry now, Mom."

Alexandra looked at the boy quickly, then down at the meatballs that she was about to put in the pan. It was only five-thirty. They always ate at six. She always made sure they did, ever since Samuel threw a fit because she was five minutes late with the food one day. Her heart started pounding in her chest.

"The food will be on the table at six, like usual. Just the way you like it, okay?" she said, with a gentle tone to her voice.

Samuel stomped his foot on the floor. Alexandra gasped and grabbed on to the counter.

Please don't be angry. Please don't throw a fit. Please don't.

"I'm hungry NOW!" he yelled. "I want meatballs NOW!"

"But sweetie...It's not ready. See, it needs to be cooked first." She took the meatballs and placed them in the pan, then set the timer. "There. Now we'll know it's done when the bell rings, alright?"

Samuel's face turned red, his eyes pitch-black. Alexandra looked at the cutting board on the counter next to him. The knife was still on top of it.

"Samuel," she said. "Calm down. Remember what we talked about. You need to try and control that anger. Don't let it control you. Do you hear me?"

But it was too late. Samuel had gone to that place where she could no longer reach him. "Samuel, please."

She stared at the knife, then made a jump for it. But it was too late. Samuel picked it up right before she managed to grab it. Now he was standing in front of her with it held high in the air.

"I'm hungry NOW!" he yelled, then swung the knife at her and cut her arm. Alexandra shrieked and pulled back. Samuel walked towards her.

"I hate you. I hate you. I hate you!" he yelled, while coming at her with the knife.

Alexandra screamed and, as he swung the knife at her again,

she moved so he wouldn't hit her. Then she ran for the door, just as Poul came through it. She threw herself into his arms.

"What's going on here?" he asked.

"Take him away from here," she cried. "I don't care where you put him. Just get him out of my house!"

Behind her, she heard the knife drop to the floor. She turned and looked at Samuel. He had tears rolling down his cheeks. "I'm sorry, Mommy," he said. Then he ran towards her and threw himself at her, trying to hug her. "I'm so sorry, Mommy. I didn't mean it. I didn't mean to do it!"

Alexandra looked down at her bleeding arm, then up at Poul. He nodded, then walked over and grabbed the boy by the arms and dragged him out of the house, while Samuel pleaded for Alexandra to change her mind.

"I'm sorry, Mommy. I'm sorry, Mommy!"

18

FEBRUARY 2014

"How on earth will you raise enough money within two hours?"

Morten was looking at me like I was insane, which I probably was. But I was determined to help this poor guy and, hopefully, save him.

"First, we need to find out how much money they need," I said. "We need to talk to the local TV station and make an announcement as quickly as possible. Could you call City Hall and tell the politicians about the situation and then ask them how much is needed to keep the place open? Then, I'll talk to the journalists."

"Got it," Morten said, and grabbed his phone. "I have to alert the station as well."

"Do you have any IT guys who can try and trace this live stream?" I asked.

Morten shook his head. "We're just a small police station. We have people in Copenhagen. I can try and contact them."

"Do that," I said, and found my own phone. I found the local TV station's number on their webpage, then called them. I told them about the story briefly and how we had very little time, then persuaded them to do a special report, *breaking news*, and let everyone know to contact me if they wanted to donate. I put the phone down and looked at Morten.

"Do you have a number?"

"Five hundred thousand kroner," he said. "Five hundred thousand and they will keep the place open."

"They're closing the place because they're short five hundred thousand kroner? That's just silly. Can't they find that in their little budget?"

Morten rubbed his temples. "Apparently not."

"Well, I guess it was the neighbor's fear and narrow-mindedness after all, huh?" I said.

"I don't like to believe so, but you might be right."

I stared at the poor guy on my computer. He was still knocking frantically on the roof of the box. "Don't use up all your oxygen too fast, sweetie," I mumbled.

I had a knot in my stomach with worry. What if we didn't find him in time? It was such a long shot. Even if we managed to raise the money - which was highly unlikely, given we had less than two hours - then how were we going to find this guy? Would the killer let him go? Or did we have to look for him ourselves?

"Who is he?" I asked again.

"I've never seen him before," Morten said.

"I thought you knew everybody."

"Well, I don't, but Allan might. He grew up on this island. He knows everybody," Morten said.

"Call him. Have him come here and take a look at the guy."

Morten smiled. "Way ahead of you. He'll be here in any second." Morten stretched his neck to the sound of a car pulling up. "As a matter of fact, he's here now."

Morten's colleague entered, took off his cap and nodded at me. "Hi Emma."

I nodded back. There wasn't time for long hellos. "This is the guy," I said and pointed at the screen.

Allan stepped forward and looked at the man kicking and knocking frantically, while screaming. I drew in a deep breath thinking that, with the rate he was going, the oxygen wouldn't last for the entire two hours.

This is insane. There is no way to save this guy!

"That's Anders Samuelsen," Allan said. "Irene Samuelsen's son. Her father used to own land on the west side of the island. When he died, she sold it all to some folks who built apartments down there for tourists. She made a fortune and never worked a day in her life."

"Anders Samuelsen," Morten repeated. "What do we know about him?"

Allan shrugged. "Not much. He kept to himself. Worked for a little while down at the harbor in one of the offices as an accountant, I believe. I had a friend working with him. He said the man was weird. Terrified of germs and touching handles. He could wash his hands for hours, my friend told me. It got really bad, as far as I know. He isolated himself and couldn't work anymore.

"Anxiety," I mumbled. "OCD."

"What did you say?" Morten asked.

"He's mentally ill, just like Susie Larsen."

19

FEBRUARY 2014

"So you're saying this guy targets the mentally ill?" Allan asked. I looked at the screen again, wondering how horrified the guy had to be...locked inside that awful box.

"I think so," I said, and looked out the window as the local TV station's van pulled up. "He has a point with all this, I think. That's why he wants to keep Hummelgaarden open."

Allan looked at Morten for answers. Morten shrugged. "A killer with a conscience, I know. It's highly unusual."

"Welcome," I said to the journalist entering my home. I showed her and her cameraman inside the kitchen and pointed at the screen.

"This is the guy we need to save. We have one hour and forty minutes to raise five hundred thousand kroner."

"We're broadcasting a special report right now," the journalist said. "We're on live in two minutes."

"Let's get it rolling then."

I flattened my hair with my hand and straightened my shirt, hoping I didn't look too much like a crazy-woman trying to scam people of their money. The journalist and cameraman got ready. I inhaled deeply to calm myself down. I could spot Anders Samuelsen on the computer out of the corner of my eye.

"And we're standing here with famous author, Emma Frost, who has taken it upon herself to raise the money that the killer has asked for to save Hummelgaarden. And Emma how much money will it take?"

"We need to raise five hundred thousand kroner to save the place and save the life of Anders Samuelsen, whom the killer has taken hostage. I want to ask everyone on the island to look into their hearts and see if they can't spare a few hundred, maybe a few thousand kroner to make sure we reach the goal. We'll be collecting the donations at City Hall, at the harbor, and at the local police station. Heck, if you see an officer, then give him some money and he'll make sure it gets here. We, as islanders, need to stick together in this matter. We can save the life of one of our neighbors or friends."

"Thank you, Emma Frost. Back to you Benny." The journalist looked at me and I could tell it was over. Then they started packing their gear down and soon they left.

"That was it," I stated. I felt strange. A man's life depended on me and my performance. It was such an awful feeling; I felt so helpless I could have cried.

"You did great, Emma," Morten said.

Allan gave me a thumps-up. "Really good, Emma."

I nodded and went back to the computer screen. I felt awful looking at him in his desperation. Morten turned on my small TV in the kitchen.

"Now we wait for the money to start rolling in," he said.

"Did you send someone to Anders Samuelsen's house?" I asked.

"We have two man searching it now," Allan said. "We're doing all we can here, alright?"

I bit my nails in distress. "I just feel like there must be more we can do."

Morten turned up the volume on the TV. I looked at it and

suddenly saw Lisa Rasmussen, a member of the Nordby City Council being interviewed. Morten opened his mouth to speak, but I stopped him.

"I want to hear what she has to say."

I turned up the volume.

"Well I for one do NOT think it's a good idea to give in to terrorists," she said. "I mean, what will he ask for next? For us to raise money so he can leave the country and go live somewhere warm and be free? No, this guy belongs in jail and I ask our local police to catch him, so we won't be in this situation again. I strongly urge people to think twice before they give money to this project. We don't even know for sure that the man is still alive, do we?"

I sunk into a chair. This was a blow in my face. I felt Morten's hand on my shoulder. "It's gonna be alright, Emma."

"Don't keep telling me it's gonna be alright. How? How is this going to ever be alright? Lisa Rasmussen basically just told everyone to not give any money for this. She just killed the guy."

"People might not listen to her at all," Morten said. "After all, she is nothing but a member of the city council."

"The most popular member of the city council this island has ever seen. The most popular politician they've ever had. The most likely to become mayor at the next election. And you think they won't listen to her? They love Lisa. They adore her and everything she's done."

"She has done some pretty awesome stuff," Allan said. "She cleaned up the city and made it less expensive to park. People love that kind of stuff."

I pulled my hair. "Argh. I'm so mad at her right now."

Morten's phone rang and he answered. When he was done talking, he looked at me.

"What?" I asked sensing bad news.

"Well City Hall has decided to not participate in the money collection. They've shut it down completely. The police station has received two hundred kroner. We got fifty down at the harbor so far, but people aren't exactly in line to donate."

"Two hundred and fifty kroner? That's all?" I asked, then looked at the clock on the live-stream. We were almost down to an hour left. I stared at Morten, feeling lost.

"What are we going to do?"

20

FEBRUARY 2014

I was biting my nails heavily now. We were all quiet in the kitchen when the phone rang again and Morten took it. I stared at the computer screen as the minutes went by and I could now see that Anders Samuelsen was having more trouble breathing. He had stopped knocking and kicking, probably because he was getting weaker by the minute.

"That was my colleagues," Morten said, as he hung up.

"They've gone through Anders Samuelsen's house twice and found nothing useful. No fingerprints or shoeprints, no blood, no sign of someone breaking and entering. Nothing."

I exhaled deeply.

"I'm sorry," Morten said.

"Well, it certainly isn't your fault. I just wish I could see a way out of this. I mean there are less than forty-five minutes till this guy runs out of air, if we are to believe the clock. There is no way we can raise the money, and we have no idea where to look for him."

Allan and Morten both nodded heavily. Morten closed his eyes. On TV, they had dropped the breaking news and were now airing some show about kite-surfers on the island. I felt sick to my stomach. How could people care this little about the life of a man? Just because they don't *give in to terrorists*? That phrase had been misused a little too much, in my opinion. It was like a pillow so they could sleep at night, wasn't it? Could that really justify killing the poor guy? I couldn't see how it could.

I, for one, wasn't just going to sit there and watch.

I got up from my chair and looked at the computer screen, then back at Morten.

"What?" he asked. "You have an idea?"

"I'm not going to just watch this man die," I said.

"No, that's clear. None of us wants that. But what do you want to do about it? What can you do? We've tried everything, I believe."

"Not everything," I said, determined.

Morten tilted his head. "What do you mean we haven't tried everything?"

"I mean there's still one thing we can do. One thing *I* can do to save Anders Samuelsen."

"I don't see what that can be. I mean, we've tried everything we can to raise the money except paying out of our own pocket..."

I smiled.

"No, Emma, no," Morten said.

"Why not?"

"Because it's a bad idea. Five hundred thousand kroner is a lot of money. It's a really bad idea. I don't think you should do that."

"But I want to. I have the money. I've made a lot on my books lately. I really don't need it. It's perfect."

"But, Emma...," Morten pleaded.

"What? What's so bad about it? I'll save the guy and save Hummelgaarden from being closed. I can't lose."

Morten exhaled. He looked to Allan for help.

"I think it's a great idea, Emma," Allan said. "I mean, if you aren't going to miss the money, that is."

"You wanted to renovate the house with that money, remember?" Morten said. "It's all your savings. What if you suddenly need it for something else, something really important?"

"What can be more important than to save this guy's life right now? I'll make more money, eventually. And the house? Well, I'll just live with it as it is. So what if the roof leaks a little in the attic? I'll fix it myself. This is more important."

"But Emma, we're not certain he'll stop here, are we? What if he wants more money from you, where will that put us? You don't know how people like that think. As soon as they discover that they can get money out of you, they'll want more. He'll kidnap more people to get you to pay. Don't you understand that?"

"Morten. You're a wonderful man, but you need to know when to shut up, which is now. I can't live with myself if I don't do this. The decision is made. I'll call Hummelgaarden right away and then have the bank transfer the money. I want you to call the local TV station and tell them I want to make a huge announcement. That way, the killer will know the money is in. Okay?"

Morten scoffed with a smile. "As you wish."

21

FEBRUARY 2014

"**W**E'VE GOT THE MONEY."

I smiled into the camera as I spoke. "I've just made sure it arrived at Hummelgaarden's account a few seconds ago. Hummelgaarden is saved."

The journalist nodded and pulled the microphone back to herself. "How did you manage to pull this off so fast?" she asked.

"Well, that doesn't matter. The important thing to focus on now is the fact that we have the money and a life will be spared."

"Rumors say you paid the amount out of your own pocket. Is that true?" the journalist asked.

"That's not important either," I said. "The money is in. That's all I have to say."

"Thank you, Emma Frost."

I thanked both of them and helped them get out the door. As soon as they were gone, I looked at the live-feed on my computer. Nothing had changed. Anders Samuelsen was still in the box. He was lying awfully still now, but I could see his chest moving up and down rapidly. He was still breathing, but only barely.

"Why hasn't he been pulled out of the box yet?" I asked, looking first at Allan, then at Morten. "Why has nothing changed? We paid the money. I announced it on TV. He must have seen it, right? He must let the guy go!"

Morten shrugged. "I don't know, Emma. I mean, how do we even know we can trust the guy? He is a killer, remember?"

"Yeah, but he promised. I mean that was the deal, wasn't it?" I found the e-mail again and read it. "It says here that, if I connect the dots, then I will win. That's what he wrote. Well I did, didn't I? I connected the dots and did as he wanted. Why isn't he doing anything? The ball is in his court now. Why isn't he doing anything, Morten?"

"I don't know, Emma."

"Oh, my God. What if we got it all wrong? What if it wasn't Hummelgaarden he wanted us to save? What if he wanted us to do something else?"

"I really don't think...," Morten sighed, and touched his unshaven chin. "We need to all calm down now, okay?"

"How am I supposed to calm down when a man is dying right here in front of me? The damn clock is still ticking. I mean, there are less than fifteen minutes left!"

"I...I...," Morten gesticulated, helplessly. His eyes were tired.

"Don't tell me you don't know. I think we've established that."

I moved the cursor across the picture to make sure it wasn't frozen or something. I updated the video but it was still the same.

"I talked to the IT guys in Copenhagen while you were on TV," Morten said. "They're working on finding the server, but I'm not sure they can find it in time."

"What the heck are we going to do now? What do we do, what do we do?" I kept saying out loud when, suddenly, a notification popped up, telling me I had received a new e-mail. With my heart racing in my chest, I opened it.

"It's from him," I almost yelled.

"What does it say?" Morten asked.

"*Congratulations. You solved the puzzle. Aren't puzzles just fun? Well, at least now you know how much people care about the mentally ill. It's scary right? Well, at least you cared enough."*

"He knows you paid the money. He might even have known you would do it all along," Morten said.

"Sounds like it," I said pensively, with my eyes fixated on the e-mail. "There's more."

"Does he say anything about Anders Samuelsen?" Allan asked.

"Damn it! He wants me to find Anders Samuelsen on my own. He says he has a clue for me. That means more games."

"What is it?" Morten asked, and looked over my shoulder.

"It looks like a riddle of some sort," I said.

22

FEBRUARY 2014

"**T**HE MAN WHO INVENTED *it doesn't want it. The man who bought it doesn't need it. The man who needs it doesn't know it. What is it?*"

I looked up from the screen and caught Morten's eyes when I had read it out loud. He looked as confused as I was.

"What the heck is that supposed to mean?" I asked.

"Let me see," Morten said.

I moved to the side so he could better see. He mumbled the words. "...doesn't want it...who bought it doesn't need it..."

"Any ideas?" I asked.

Morten shook his head. "None whatsoever. Riddles were never my thing."

"Mine either," I said.

"Allan?"

"Don't ask me."

I leaned back with a deep sigh. "How on earth are we supposed to figure this out with less than fifteen minutes left?"

My brain was working overtime as I stared at the riddle in front of me. "There has to be someone who can solve this. Don't you have someone in the force who can help?"

"I'll make some calls," Morten said, and left the kitchen with the phone to his ear.

"Me too," Allan said, and picked up his phone as well.

My hands were sweaty. I watched the riddle in front of me, trying desperately to figure out what the killer meant, what he wanted me to do. I was breathing heavily, my heart beating so fast it almost hurt in my chest. I was on the verge of breaking down and crying. There was no way I could solve this in time. There was no way I could save this guy, was there? I looked at the live feed where Anders Samuelsen lay quietly in the box with his eyes closed. He was still breathing, but that wouldn't last long.

I rubbed my temples and closed my eyes to better concentrate. This was, after all, just a riddle, wasn't it? It was something made to be solved. With the right brain you could find the answer. But, unfortunately, mine wasn't constructed in the right way to solve it. At least I didn't think so, until something suddenly hit me. It literally felt like I was struck by lightning. I opened my eyes and stared at Anders Samuelsen and the box he was in.

"The box," I mumbled.

I rose from my chair while the thoughts ran through my mind. "The man who invented it doesn't want it. The man who bought it doesn't need it. The man who needs it doesn't know it," I mumbled, while biting my lip.

This has to be it. It just has to be. Please let this be it!

"Morten?" I called, then walked out in the hallway to find him. He was still on the phone. I signaled he should hang up.

"Call me back if you find a solution," he said, then put the phone down.

"You've got it?" he asked. "You found the answer?"

It bit my lip. "I think I have, but I might be wrong."

Oh, God, what if I'm wrong?

"It's better than nothing," Morten said.

"What's going on?" Allan asked, and walked closer.

"Emma thinks she might know the answer to the riddle."

"Really?"

"Yes, but I have no time to explain," I said, and grabbed my winter coat and put on my boots. "I'll tell you everything in the car. Allan can you stay here with Victor? He's playing in the yard. Just make sure he's safe, will you?"

Allan nodded. "Got it."

"What about Maya?" Morten asked, when we ran for the car.

"She's in town with her grandmother."

We jumped in the police car and Morten put the key in. "So where are we going?"

"To the cemetery."

23

FEBRUARY 2014

"Why are we going to the cemetery?" Morten asked, puzzled, as we drove across town with the siren blaring.

"It's a coffin," I said, while holding on to the handle in the car when Morten took a sharp turn.

"Hold on," Morten said, and turned again. The tires skidded off the road in the snow. Morten turned the wheel and got the car back on track and continued.

"A coffin, huh? Yeah, I can see how that makes sense. I mean to the riddle and everything. The man who invented it, doesn't want it; no, of course not. No one wants a coffin, so he sells it to someone who doesn't need it, because you have to be dead to need it. And the man who needs it doesn't know he does, since he is dead. Am I right?"

"Something like that," I said. "At least, I hope that's the right solution. I'm really scared that it's not. This is our final chance. If we don't find Anders Samuelsen in the cemetery, then it's over."

Morten cleared his throat. "I know," he said with a quiet voice. "I'm sure it's the right answer."

He didn't sound convincing and that made my stomach turn.

Please, dear God, let this be it; let us find him or I will never be able to live with myself!

Morten called for backup and an ambulance as we drove into the cemetery and he stopped the car in front of a huge pile of snow.

"Let's go," I said, and jumped out of the car.

I stormed across the graveyard, frantically searching for something, anything, that could point to where Anders Samuelsen was. Desperately, I turned around, looked in all directions, but nothing. All the graves looked the same. All of them were covered in snow.

"You look in that direction!" I yelled, and ran the opposite way.

"Damn the snow," I mumbled. "It's covering all tracks. Everything out here looks the same."

Please help me. Please give me a sign, a path, anything to go by. Where is that coffin? Is it even here?

Morten ran up behind me. He was panting as he spoke. "There is nothing here. Do you think he buried him or what are we looking for?"

I was on the verge of bursting into tears, but held it back as much as I could. "I don't know," I said.

That was when I spotted it. Right in front of us, between two bushes, I saw something. It looked like footprints in the snow. A long line of them.

"When did it last snow?" I asked.

"Two days ago, I think," Morten said.

"Bingo."

I ran towards the tracks and followed them to a grave. There was a huge pile of snow on top of it, but something was off about it.

"Look at that. It looks like the snow has been shoveled onto the grave, doesn't it? The snow doesn't look the same as it does on the other graves, does it?"

"I think you're right; it's mixed with dirt," Morten said. "It's been dug up recently."

Morten fell to his knees and started digging with his bare hands. I turned to look around me and spotted a shovel leaning on the wall of the church next to the cemetery. I ran to get it and, seconds later, Morten had dug a pretty big hole in the ground. Suddenly, the shovel hit something.

"I think this is it!" I yelled.

Morten continued to dig around it and soon a black coffin showed up. We heard voices behind us and more policemen came running to help us pull it up from the hole in the ground. They used a crowbar to open the lid.

"Please hurry. Please hurry," I said.

The lid came off and I could now see Anders Samuelsen. He was lying completely still and was very pale. Morten leaned over his body. He felt for a pulse. In the distance I could hear the ambulance getting closer.

Morten's face looked serious. "I can't feel it," he said.

My heart was beating rapidly. Two paramedics came to the scene. Morten and I moved away and let them take care of it. I leaned on Morten's shoulder and finally dared to let the tears roll.

Please let him be alive.

24

FEBRUARY 2014

Anders Samuelsen was dreaming when he felt the pain in his chest. It was a nice dream. It had removed all the anxiety and fear that his life had been so filled with for the last many years. For the first time since he could remember, he was at peace. His dream was calm and he didn't want to let go of it again, but the choice wasn't his.

He felt the pain in his chest once again and opened his eyes with a loud gasp. That was when he saw her for the first time. She was standing a few steps behind the many yellow jackets who were frantically pushing his chest, yelling at him, and now using a defibrillator on him. But Anders didn't look at them, nor did he care what they did or what happened to him. All he cared about was that beautiful face behind them all, the woman with the beautiful eyes, looking at him with worry.

Anders had been afraid all of his life, but for once, he opened his eyes without being struck by those taunting emotions that had destroyed so much for him for so long. Looking into her eyes, he felt calm. He knew they were all working to save his life, and somehow he knew he had died down in that box and was now being revived.

He knew he had gone through his own worst nightmare of being buried alive and slowly losing air, but somehow, none of that mattered right now. He was alive.

"He's breathing!" someone yelled.

Anders smiled and didn't take his eyes off of the woman while they carried him up on a stretcher and started rolling him towards an ambulance.

All of his life, he had feared being sick, feared having to be taken to the hospital in an ambulance; he had feared dying.

But not anymore. He had tried it and it wasn't all that bad.

The woman ran next to the stretcher and Anders looked at her with a blissful smile. He even reached out his hand towards her, right before he was pushed inside the ambulance where they did all kinds of things to him that he didn't care about. The last thing he saw as they closed the doors was her. She was standing on the gravel outside looking at him...looking so beautiful.

My angel.

He heard more voices in the distance, then felt the ambulance take off. In the hospital, he was examined and treated for hours and hours. The doctor spoke to him and so did the nurses, and Anders answered the best he could, still with the blissful smile on his face.

I beat death. Nothing can beat me now. I'm invincible! I've never felt more alive in my life!

Two days passed in the hospital bed where he slowly got better and better. He joked with the nurses and laughed with the other patients, who found him to be entertaining and funny. But, best of all, Anders was happy. For the first time in his life, he wasn't afraid. He wasn't terrified, constantly thinking about what could possibly go wrong, what could possibly make him sick or hurt him in any way.

He was finally free.

On the second day, a police offer named Morten Bredballe came to his bed and asked him a ton of questions that Anders answered happily.

"Did you see the man who did this to you?"

"I did," he answered, smiling. "He was driving the cab I was in when he kidnapped me. I got a very good look at his face before he sedated me."

Anders saw how the officer's face lit up. "That's excellent," he said. "Did you know him?"

"I felt like I had seen him before, but I didn't know where. I don't go out much. At least, I didn't used to. Now, I think I will. Now, I think I'm going to go out every day and enjoy this beautiful world. This island has so much to offer, do you realize that? So much we don't appreciate. I think it's about time we all start living a little, don't you?"

The officer looked at him, puzzled. Anders didn't care.

"There was a woman at the cemetery when you found me. Who was she?" he asked.

"Who, Emma?" Officer Bredballe asked.

"Emma, what a delightful name. Almost angelic."

"I guess so. I never thought of that," the officer said. "She's a writer. She's actually the one who figured out where to look for you. She's been very worried about you and whether you'd make it or not."

Anders couldn't stop smiling. "I think I'll have to give her my thanks once I'm out of here."

The officer smiled. "Well, first of all, get well. That's what's important now. As soon as you're well enough, we'll send a sketch artist out to draw a picture of the guy who put you in that box. We want him in jail as quickly as possible."

25

FEBRUARY 2014

I was so exhausted. After finding the guy alive, I went straight to bed when I got home and stayed in it for two days. Luckily, I had my mother to take care of the kids and, even though I knew it would be hard on Victor, I felt like I needed this. I had to do it. I needed a break from the world.

Morten came to visit every day and even stayed the night. He made me feel good. He made sure I got something to eat - something real and not the strange food that my mother served me - and he spoiled me with chocolates and red wine.

On the night of the second day, he lay in my bed with me and held me tight in his arms while he told me what Anders Samuelsen had told him at the hospital earlier that day.

"It was strange, 'cause the guy seemed to smile through everything. It was like he was in a world of his own. But he did tell me that he knew what the guy looked like. So, as soon as we get the sketch done, we'll go public with it and nail him within just a few hours."

"Someone is feeling confident," I said, as I ate a chocolate.

"This is a small island. You can't hide for long," Morten said. "We'll get him. I can feel it in my guts."

"Your police-guts," I said with a smile.

"Yup."

Morten turned on his side and kissed my neck. He leaned over and continued down. He undid the buttons on my very un-sexy pajamas, then opened the shirt and kissed my breasts. I closed my eyes and put my hands around his neck and pulled him closer. He removed my hands, then pulled off my pants and undressed himself. Now we were both naked in the bed. We lay entangled with legs between each other's, face to face and he pulled the covers over us. I laughed and kissed his nose, his lips, then closed my eyes as he entered me. I moaned and, for just a few seconds, let go of control.

When I opened my eyes, I stared directly into his and saw the love for me in them. This was a beautiful moment, one I wanted to last.

Afterwards, we lay with his head on the pillow, his arm around my neck, the back of my head resting on his chest. He gave me my glass of wine and I sipped it, feeling better than I had in days.

"Guess it was just what the doctor ordered," I said with a smile.

Morten kissed my forehead, then sipped his wine.

"So, you think it's over now?" I asked.

"What is?"

"The killer? You think he's done?"

Morten ate a piece of chocolate. "Sure. He got what he wanted didn't he?"

"You think that was all that he wanted? To save Hummelgaarden?" I asked, puzzled.

Morten shrugged. "It's all he demanded, isn't it?"

"Guess so. But I can't stop thinking..."

"You think way too much."

"Okay, I'll give you that, but still."

"Still what, my little Sherlock?"

"He killed two women, buried a guy alive, and nearly killed him as well. All for what? Five hundred thousand kroner? It sounds a little extreme to me."

Morten nodded. "Sure. But, who knows why people do stuff like this? He's a psychopath, and who knows what goes on inside of their minds?"

I exhaled and sipped more wine. "I guess you're right."

"Don't worry, sweetheart. We'll find him and then it'll all be over. Trust me. We have a team from Esbjerg who has come over here to help us catch him. I give him three days. Tops."

"I sure hope you're right."

26

APRIL 2007

Alexandra closed her eyes and leaned back in her chair. She was sitting on the porch in her backyard, enjoying the few rays of sun that spring had brought with promise of summer around the corner. She breathed in deeply and hummed a little as she exhaled again. Oh, how she enjoyed the peace.

It had been a year since Poul took Samuel away and put him in boarding school. And, even if Alexandra wasn't happy to admit it, she had enjoyed every minute of the peace since...immensely.

Samuel had been home on vacation for Christmas, but other than that she hadn't seen him. She missed her son, of course she did, and she hated the fact that it had to be this way, but oh, the peace and quiet inside of her was all worth it. After so many years of fearing the boy's rage and tantrums, she was now, finally, living her own life again, not constantly afraid to say or do something wrong. And the boy was getting a wonderful education. Poul kept telling her so and she knew he was right. Herlufsholm Boarding School was the best school in the country. Samuel was among sons of big-shot CEOs and the Danish aristocracy. It was a school with great discipline and many traditions. They could take Samuel's hand and straighten him up. She knew they could.

It was the best for everybody, she kept telling herself, mostly to try and drown out that nagging doubt and feeling of guilt that was growing inside of her. Samuel had seemed fine at Christmas. He had been very quiet and mostly stayed in his room. Not once did he have one of his tantrums. He had been a completely different son.

Poul and Alexandra's marriage was doing slightly better as well. Alexandra now had the energy to actually be a wife to her husband and Poul had stopped spending all his time in the garage. They had somehow found each other again and it felt so good. It was actually so great that Alexandra had become pregnant again and they were expecting a little girl in three months.

Alexandra touched her stomach gently and caressed it, thinking about the little girl growing inside of her and how wonderful it was for them to be able to start all over, even if she was now at the age of forty-two.

"This time, it's going to be perfect," she said with a secretive smile, while the baby kicked on the inside. "I'm not making the same mistakes again."

Poul appeared on the porch with a glass of juice that he put on the table in front of her. She looked up and smiled.

"Is she kicking again?" he asked.

Alexandra nodded. "You want to feel her?"

"Sure."

Poul put his hand gently on Alexandra's big stomach and felt the baby kick. Alexandra laughed. "Look," she said and pointed at a small bump that was moving across the stomach. "The doctor said that's her ankle."

"She's getting big, huh?" Poul said.

"I'm not sure there's enough room for her in there to stay another three months," Alexandra laughed.

"Well, Samuel was ten days late, so don't get your hopes up of this one arriving on time," Poul said.

Then they both went quiet.

"You do realize what day it is today, right?" Alexandra asked.

Poul nodded. "I know. I know." He bit his lip.

"He's turning eleven, Poul. We should at least call him at the school."

Poul's eyes were filled. "I don't know what to say to him anymore. I mean, he hurt you, Alex. You still have a scar from where he cut you."

Alexandra dropped her head. She felt like crying, but didn't. "I know. But let's at least call him. I don't like the fact that he might be lonely at that school...if no one celebrates him. Plus, I feel really bad that we've told the school to keep him all summer like last year. I know it's too much for us to handle him now that we have the baby and all, but still..."

Poul nodded. "I guess you're right." Poul sighed and went inside the house. He came back with the phone in his hand. He looked at it like he needed time to find the courage. Then, he handed it to Alexandra.

"Here. You do it."

She took it. "Okay." She felt the heavy phone in her hand and got ready to dial the number, when suddenly the phone rang. She looked up at Poul.

"It's the school."

"I'll take it," Poul said, and grabbed the phone from her hand.

Alexandra felt her heart beat faster as she looked how Poul's expression changed drastically during the conversation. She could see in his eyes that it was bad. A thousand fearful thoughts ran through her mind.

Oh, Samuel. What did you do now?

"We'll be right there," Poul said, and hung up.

Alexandra stared into his eyes.

"It was the headmaster," he said, his voice heavy with sadness. "Samuel is in the hospital. He tried to kill himself."

27

FEBRUARY 2014

So, according to Morten, it was all over, right? That was what I kept telling myself, as I slowly returned to my everyday life, getting the kids to school, working on my book, and baking. A couple more days had passed since I pulled Anders Samuelsen out of the ground and I was told he had now been discharged from the hospital. The local newspaper and the TV station were all over him and I had seen and read more than one interview with the guy who beat death.

This morning, he was on the front cover of *Fanoe Xpress* again. This time in a picture of him skydiving from an airplane over the island. I chuckled and picked up the paper from the table. In a smaller picture underneath - taken after he had landed - Anders Samuelsen was smiling widely.

"Dying was the best thing that ever happened to me," he stated. "I have never felt more alive."

I laughed and read the article where he told about how dying and seeing the light had made him realize that he hadn't been living at all. That dying wasn't something we should be afraid of. It had been wonderful, so warm and peaceful and he was actually looking forward to going back once his time was up.

"But apparently, that isn't yet," he said to end the interview.

My mom walked into the kitchen just as I finished the article. "Can you believe this guy?" I said, and showed her the picture. "Since he was discharged from the hospital two days ago, he has been skydiving, bungee-jumping and started doing motocross. It's insane. I mean, before all this happened, the guy suffered from anxiety so bad that he was declared unfit to work."

"Well, I guess the county will have to reevaluate him soon and then he'll lose his benefits," my mom said.

"Then he can go get a job like the rest of us," I said, and pushed the button on the coffeemaker.

My mother looked at me. "You don't have a real job."

"I beg your pardon?"

"You know what I mean," she said, and found some of her gluten-free bread that she put in the toaster.

"I'm afraid I really don't," I said. "The last time I checked, I wrote books, which takes a lot of time and effort."

My mother scoffed. "Well in the time I've been here, you haven't been working many hours."

I shook my head. I hated the fact that what she said got to me like this. I felt so aggravated. If it had been anyone else besides my own mother, I wouldn't have cared what they thought, but with her, I did. She could really get to me with her words. I closed my eyes and swallowed my pride, reminding myself that she was only here for a short period of time, and I would soon have my house to myself again.

Her bread was done and my mother picked it up from the toaster. She put cheese on both pieces of bread and put them on two plates. She saw me staring.

"I promised Maya to make one for her as well," she said. "So you don't have to prepare anything for her. I'm making one of my healthy smoothies for her as well. She likes them."

My mother took her laptop and sat at the table with a cup of white tea. I poured myself some coffee and sipped it. I thought about Morten and wondered if today was going to be the day they caught the killer. I hated that they didn't have him yet. They'd tried to trace his e-mails and the link to the video of Anders Samuelsen in the box, but had no success yet. Furthermore, they had a sketch made from Anders Samuelsen's description, but it wasn't very good. The guy had long hair and glasses, but other than that, Anders hadn't been able to describe many details. Not even the color of the eyes. It was really disappointing to me. Morten had told me they would find him, but I had my serious doubts. This guy was way too intelligent to get caught. He knew there was a possibility that Anders was going to survive and that he would be able to tell us what the killer looked like. He wasn't going to risk being recognized so, of course, he had changed his looks somehow...maybe even worn a disguise when kidnapping Anders Samuelsen.

My mom was chuckling, then tapping on her keyboard.

"What's so funny?" I asked.

"Oh it's just Arne. He's really funny."

I sat next to my mother and looked at the screen. "You're Facebook friends with my mailman?"

"Yes," she said, laughing again at something he had written to her in a private message. "Oh, is that going to be weird for you?"

"I guess not," I lied. I thought it was weird already.

"Good. He really makes me laugh, you know. I like him."

I sipped my coffee. "As in like him because he's funny or as in *like-like* him?" I asked, slightly terrified.

"Well, I don't quite know yet. But we're going out tonight so, after that, I'll be able to tell you."

I almost choked on my coffee. "You're going out with the mailman?"

"Don't call him that. That's patronizing. His name is Arne and he's a very nice man who knows how to treat a woman right."

28

FEBRUARY 2014

Dagmar Madsen bit her nails. She looked at the carpet in the waiting room while feeling anxious. Not because she was about to see a new doctor, she had done that so many times before, but because she was afraid he might find out about her.

Dagmar had been diagnosed with many kinds of mental illnesses over the years: bipolar disorder, anxiety, depression, schizophrenia, eating disorders, you name it. She knew everything there was to know about mental illnesses and was a walking encyclopedia when it came to medicine. She knew all of the symptoms and knew exactly what to say to the doctor to make him give her the drugs she wanted.

A door opened and a friendly face appeared. "Dagmar Madsen?" The woman approached her and shook her hand.

Dagmar got up, her eyes still avoiding the doctor's. Not because she was nervous, no, Dagmar made her eyes wander to be convincing.

"Come on in."

Dagmar followed the doctor into her office. Just like all the other doctors' offices, it was nicely decorated with nature paintings and plants in the corners. It had a nice and calm ambiance meant to make the patient feel calm and peaceful. The doctor asked Dagmar to sit on the couch. She looked through the papers that Dagmar had filled out in the waiting room and flipped a couple of pages while Dagmar continued to bite her nails until one of them started bleeding.

"Have you been to a psychiatrist before?"

Dagmar cleared her throat and nodded.

"Well, good. I see that you've been diagnosed with bipolar disorder?"

"Yes. That's why I'm here. I need to renew my prescription."

"Okay, well let's talk a little first. So why did you leave your old psychiatrist?"

Dagmar's eyes flickered. She was well-prepared for this question. They all asked the same. The truth was that she hadn't left her old psychiatrist. She hadn't left any of them. For the time being, she was seeing six different psychiatrists.

Unlike many other psychiatric patients, Dagmar didn't mind taking her medicine. As a matter of fact, she loved it so much, she took twice, sometimes triple the dose she was supposed to. It helped her calm down and sometimes drugged her just enough to get through the day. But, of course, the doctors could never know that. Once they refused to prescribe more to her than what she was supposed to have, she found another to give her more.

"I need lithium," she said, while the fingers on her right hand drummed on her thigh. One of them was still bleeding. It made the act more believable.

"So, that is what you used to get?" the psychiatrist asked.

"Yes. If I could get some antidepressant too, then that would be good. It helps with the restlessness that I get from the Lithium. And maybe a nonbenzodiazepine, like Zolpidem, to take care of the insomnia."

The psychiatrist looked at Dagmar. "You seem to know a lot about medicine?" she asked.

"I've been sick for many years," Dagmar said.

"Have you ever considered combining the medicine with therapy?"

"That's not for me," Dagmar said, and looked down at the carpet again. She knew this point in the conversation very well. The doctors always said the same thing. All she needed was to stay calm. As long as the doctor didn't try and contact her previous doctor, then she was good. All she needed was that small yellow note with the right words on it to give her the drugs she needed. Especially, the Zolpidem was important. Dagmar had gotten addicted to those. She loved the way she dozed off after taking a couple of them. It made her go numb and sometimes even forget everything the next morning.

The psychiatrist wrote on her notepad. She looked up and handed Dagmar the prescription. Dagmar took it and held it tightly in her hands.

Finally. Finally. Oh boy.

"You do know that Zolpidem, taken in too high a dose, can cause amnesia," the doctor said. "It can also be fatal taken with other medications that cause drowsiness...and don't drink alcohol. Never take any more than it says on the bottle, okay? An overdose could kill you."

"Oh, I know," Dagmar said with a smile. Her hands were shaking in withdrawal. She hadn't had anything today at all since all her bottles were empty and her usual doctor refused to prescribe more. Dagmar got up from her chair, then shook the doctor's hand.

"Thank you, thank you," she said, then rushed out the doctor's office.

29

FEBRUARY 2014

I t was late in the afternoon and getting dark as Dagmar took the ferry back to Fanoe Island and went to the pharmacy, before she hurried home to her small apartment in Nordby that was located in an old building right above a hairdresser.

She opened the door and rushed inside. She took off her jacket and her boots, then pulled out the bottles from the small plastic bag. The lady at the pharmacy had looked at her like she was crazy when she had handed her the prescription.

"Didn't you just get a new dose last week?" she asked.

Sometimes Dagmar really hated living on a small island. It hadn't taken her long to figure out that she had to find doctors on the mainland to help her get her prescriptions, but maybe it was about time she started using their pharmacies as well. She didn't like the way the lady behind the counter had looked at her. No, it was time to change her pharmacy as well.

"Next time," she mumbled, and looked at the many bottles on her kitchen table. There was enough for at least a couple of weeks. It made her feel calm. She would probably have to go all the way to

Vejle next time to find a psychiatrist who would give her more medication, but she'd cross that bridge when she got to it.

She didn't understand all their concerns, though. Dagmar knew everything she needed to know about her medicine. She knew exactly how much she could take without it being dangerous. She knew which kind of pills went well with others and which didn't. She was an expert, one that had actually tried it all on her own body. She was very controlled and made sure all she did was to get sedated enough to forget all those thoughts she couldn't get rid of. But she had never taken too much. And she never would. She was way too experienced for that.

Dagmar grabbed a glass and filled it with tap water. Then, she took her bottle of pills and took out three. Yes, it was three times as many as prescribed, but she knew she could take it. If she took four, it would be bad, but she didn't.

Dagmar placed the pills on the table in front of her in a row and sat down with her glass of water. She felt sad for a second, thinking about her twin brother, who had been killed when they were just fourteen. Their stepdad had beaten him to death while Dagmar was watching. The stepdad had done his time, ten years in jail, and now he was out and had started a new family with another woman. Meanwhile, Dagmar's mother had killed herself after her brother's death and now Dagmar had no one left. It saddened her deeply, but the pills helped her to not get too sad. Sometimes, they even made her forget completely. She needed that. She needed to forget. She needed to remain sedated in order to make it through the day. Otherwise, she could only think about her brother and how unfair it all was and how alone she was in this forsaken world.

Dagmar felt the heavy sadness weigh her down and picked up a pill with the intention of taking it, when there was a knock on her door. She put the pill in her mouth and swallowed it. There was another knock. Dagmar didn't know what to do. She never had guests. She had no friends and no family.

Another knock.

This time it sounded urgent. She got up. Someone probably had the wrong address or something. She walked to the door and opened it. Outside stood a man whose face she knew very well.

The man smiled diabolically, then pulled a knife and placed it on her throat while pushing her backwards into the apartment. He slammed the door with his foot behind him. Dagmar was stunned. Perplexed. She had no idea what was going on.

"What...?"

She tried to speak, but he pressed the knife towards her skin.

"Shh," he said.

"I don't understand."

The man smashed his fist into her face and she felt an excruciating pain. Dagmar screamed and fell to the ground. The man hit her again and again, plunging his fist into her face and body, till she was so beaten, she couldn't scream anymore. Then he pulled her by the hair and sat her in a chair. Dagmar moaned and tried to focus, but everything remained a blur.

The man then took all of her pill bottles and placed them on the table in front of her, one after another. She heard the well-known sound of them being opened, then felt how he opened her mouth forcefully and started pouring pills on her tongue. She wanted to protest; she wanted to stop him, but she couldn't. Everything was so unreal and so blurry now, she had no idea how to stop him or for what reason she would. He would only hit her again. Dagmar felt water in her mouth and started to swallow in order to not get suffocated. She gasped for air and coughed. The water stopped and she caught her breath again. She opened her eyes and saw the man empty the bottle of Zolpidem into his hand.

"Please, don't," she mumbled between coughs. "That many pills will kill me."

The man laughed and pulled out a brown bottle of whiskey from his long black coat.

"No, they won't. But this might."

30

FEBRUARY 2014

I was listening to my mother getting ready upstairs, playing eighties music and trying to out sing Diana Ross on *Upside Down*. I wasn't angry; I mean, how could I be? It was her life and if she wanted to date my mailman, then there wasn't much I could do about it, was there?

Still, I felt awful.

Why? Well, I just didn't enjoy the idea of my mother with another man. She belonged with my dad and I realized as I sat there in the kitchen staring at a blank page on my computer trying to write my next book while the kids did their homework, that I had somehow thought that was why she had come back. To get my father back.

I sighed and typed a couple of words, then deleted them again. I couldn't believe myself. Was this really true? Was I dreaming of my parents getting back together again after all these years?

Maya was struggling with her math and asked for my help. I showed her how to solve the problem. It was just my luck that I had always been excellent at math.

"I still don't get it," Maya said.

I explained it to her again. She looked at me like I was crazy. Guess I hadn't been able to pass down my good math genes to her. I looked at Victor, who was reading a book about the French Revolution. He seemed to be dwelling on the pictures that I found extremely gross. It had been a bad day for him at school. I had received a call from his principal telling me that Victor had made a report with highly inappropriate details, which he had presented for the class today. He had a slideshow and everything, showing mostly decapitated heads. When the teacher told him to stop, Victor started arguing that this was an important event in history and continued. In the end, the teacher pulled the plug on the slideshow and asked Victor to sit down. That was when Victor had started screaming hysterically. The teacher had then grabbed his shoulder and that had only made things worse. Victor didn't like to be touched, so he had screamed even louder and started hitting. The teacher claimed Victor hit him deliberately in the face, but Victor explained he had just pushed him away to get his hands off of him. Now, the principal thought Victor might be too much for the school to handle and recommended that we start looking for another school, one that maybe knew how to deal with *his kind of mental problems.*

I had no idea where to look for a school like that. I wasn't even sure it existed. I had worked on it all afternoon, checking the web and calling the school, which referred me to City Hall.

"It really isn't our problem," the school's secretary had said. "If the child is too difficult, then we leave it to the county to find another place for him or her."

Too difficult? Who are you calling too difficult?

"The county will appoint a social worker for you to handle the case."

I had hung up feeling like screaming. My son needed a social worker? Was that what it had come to?

"What about the next one?" Maya asked now and showed me another problem she couldn't solve.

"I'm not going to do all of your homework for you," I said. "Try it and see if you can solve it on your own, then I'll help."

Maya exhaled, annoyed. "It's like you don't even want to help me."

"I am helping you by not solving everything for you. You're supposed to be able to do this on your own in class. If I do all your homework, how are you going to handle a test in school?"

Maya rolled her eyes at me. "It's so easy for you to say," she grumbled.

"Maya. I'm not doing it for you!" I said, a little harsher than I meant to.

"Geez. There is no reason to scream," she said, and got up from her chair. She took her math book. "If you don't want to help me. Just say so."

Before I could answer, she had stormed out the door while the tones of the Captain and Tennille singing *Do That to Me One More Time* along with my mother hit me from upstairs.

31

FEBRUARY 2014

"So what do we do, huh buddy?" I asked Victor.

As usual, he didn't answer. He flipped a page in his book. I felt a sadness inside. It was just so difficult. I had no idea how to help him. Like any mother, I only wanted what was best for my boy, but since he had no straight diagnosis, there was simply no help to get. I had been to every doctor and specialist and they all had different opinions. Some said Asperger's, others said he was slightly bipolar, but I didn't believe any of it. I had tried everything anyway, but no medication had helped and no therapy. It was simply frustrating. Moving to the island had definitely helped him improve. He was happier and he went longer between his seizures and tantrums. But, it was like it wasn't quite enough.

I drew in a deep breath and wondered what was supposed to become of him. How was he supposed to get by in this world? They were going to crush him. Putting him in an institution made no sense, since he could do everything himself. He was just so absent-minded. He lived in a world of his own. A world I believed was filled with magic and wonders none of us would ever have the imagination or even the intelligence to understand.

But the kids in school were beginning to realize that he was different and I was afraid of him being bullied. I had no idea if he himself realized that he was different, but at some point, he had to know.

"Do you like your school Victor?" I asked.

He nodded.

"Why? What do you like about it?"

"I like that I get to read books while the other kids have to listen to the teacher," he said, without looking up from the book.

"They let you do that, huh?"

"Yes. It's nice. I know everything the teacher is saying and, that way, I won't interrupt him, he says."

I bit my lip wondering if the teacher was just placing Victor in the corner with a book so he didn't have to deal with him, or if it was so he wouldn't be bored because he already knew everything.

"Maybe we should find you a new school, huh buddy? Would you like that?" I asked.

"No," he answered. "I like my school."

"Okay," I said. "But then you'll have to go by their rules, do you understand? You can't show the class bloody pictures of decapitated heads."

"Why not? It's history?"

"Because it's inappropriate."

"I don't understand."

"I know you don't. But when a teacher asks you to stop, you stop. You can't fight with them, okay? If you promise to behave, then I'll see what I can do to help you stay. You might have to see a therapist or something for a little while if the county asks you to."

Victor didn't answer. He flipped another page and continued reading. "No more bringing these books to school, alright? We keep them at home."

I got up from my chair and started on the lasagna I was planning on serving for dinner. I had invited my dad over since my mom was going out. I chopped onions and made the meat sauce, then I put it all together with my secret ingredient, a cheesy Morney sauce and put it in the oven. I wondered if I should make a salad as well when I heard the doorbell and went to open it. Outside stood the mailman. He was nicely dressed and looked very different from how I usually saw him. Almost handsome.

"I'm coming," my mother chirped from upstairs. She made her entrance the way I was certain she had planned it in her head and walked slowly down the stairs in her blue dress.

She looked amazing.

"Wow, Mom. You...you look really great," I said, when she came closer.

"Thank you, darling," she said, and touched my cheek gently.

"I concur," the mailman said and grabbed her hand and kissed the back of it. "You look absolutely stunning."

My mother giggled like a schoolgirl. It was all a little absurd, I thought to myself. My mother with her weird face that was constantly smiling and now this guy who was my mailman looking like a George Clooney clone. I couldn't really grasp it. But, as if that wasn't strange enough, suddenly I spotted my dad coming up the driveway towards the house. He paused when he saw her.

"Ulla?"

32

FEBRUARY 2014

"**U**LLA?"
        My dad looked at my mom like he couldn't believe his own eyes. He was early. At least half an hour too early.

"Bengt?" my mother said. For the first time since she got there, I saw her facial expression change slightly. Her eyes looked sad. "I didn't expect to see you here?"

"I invited him since you were going out," I said. "He usually comes here several times a week."

My father couldn't take his eyes off of my mother. "You look... You look really great Ulla. Emma did tell me you were in town, but I didn't expect to see you here...like this." His eyes then turned to glance at the handsome mailman. "Oh...You're...You're going out?"

My mother nodded. Arne held his hand out. "Arne," he said when my dad took it. "I...We were just..."

"Sure," my dad said, half choked. "Go have fun. By all means, have a great time."

Arne took my mom's hand and they started walking. My mother threw my dad a guilty look.

"See you later, Bengt."

"Yeah. Yes, of course. See you another time."

It was heartbreaking to watch. I put my arm around my dad's shoulder while we watched my mom and Arne take off in his small Toyota. Not exactly the kind of car my mother was used to.

"I'm sorry you had to see that," I said. "I thought they would be out of the house by the time you got here."

We walked back into the house.

"It's my own fault for being early. I know you told me your mother was going out. I just missed you guys so much I thought... well, I thought she had left long ago and I certainly didn't know that she was going out with someone. Well to be completely honest, maybe I was hoping to run into her. She looked really great, don't you think? Really great..."

I found a bottle of red wine on the counter when we entered the kitchen and opened it. I poured my dad a glass. "Here."

"Thanks, honey." He sipped it while I looked at him with my heart broken. I couldn't believe he had to see this. It was awful.

"Where are the kids?" he asked.

"Victor was just here. Maya got mad about her homework and is probably in her room, rolling her eyes at me."

"Well it's nice to know that some things stay the same."

I chuckled. "I guess so. Well, there are still twenty minutes till dinner if you want to go up and talk to them. They've missed you."

My dad got up from his chair. "I bet they have," he said with a forced smile. I could still see the hurt in his eyes.

He left and I poured myself a glass of wine and sat down at my computer. I called Morten to hear if we were still on for dinner and he told me he was on his way. I closed my document that I had tried to work on all day, but didn't succeed in writing as much as a sentence. Then I went on Facebook and scrolled through my news-feed. As usual...nothing new. I watched a video of cats hiding in funny places then another about dogs wearing hats, then decided it was a waste of my time and closed the tab. I noticed I had a few new e-mails and opened my mailbox to check what they were. Mostly spam, but there was one that made my heart stop.

No. No. Not again!

It was another one without a sender or subject. My hand started shaking as I moved the mouse and clicked to open it.

33

FEBRUARY 2014

Dear Emma, You didn't really think it was over, did you? I don't think you did. You did great on your first assignment, so now it's time for your next. See the picture at the bottom of this e-mail? This shows a woman. She is in trouble and only you can save her. She has taken way too many pills and swallowed them with alcohol. Not good, right? I know. It's really bad. The mixture in her stomach will kill her if you don't find her as soon as possible. But where is she hiding, Emma? Where is she? It's time for another round of Hide and Go Seek.

I scrolled frantically down the e-mail and found the picture. Then, I gasped. It showed a badly-bruised woman who was lying on what looked like a wooden floor with her eyes closed. Next to her were five bottles of pills. All empty.

"Oh my God," I mumbled. "Oh my good God."

I picked up my phone and called Morten and a few minutes later he was standing in my kitchen.

"I'm so sorry," he said, and hugged me. "I was so sure it was over."

"Me too," I said, feeling the knot in my stomach grow. "What do we do?"

Morten pulled up a chair and sat next to me. He read the e-mail, then looked at the picture.

"It doesn't look like he has any demands like last time," I said.

"What are those attachments?" Morten asked.

"I don't know. I didn't see them until now," I said, and clicked on the first. "It looks like statistics."

"What kind of statistics?"

"Overdose. Like this one. It's a statistic from last year about mentally ill people who have died from an overdose of their medication."

"Okay, so like last time, he wants us to focus on something. He wants our attention," Morten said pensively.

"So we'll have to assume that the woman in the picture is another mentally ill person, right?" I asked.

"I think so," Morten said. "And he's made her take all of her medicine in order to bring focus on how often mentally ill patients die from overdoses."

I nodded and looked at the picture. It was hard to look at the woman, so I tried to focus on the details in her surroundings, instead. But it was difficult, since all we could see was the floor and the bottles. Behind her was something blue – it looked like a big heavy curtain, but that could be anywhere.

"Okay, so he's made his point...what do we do now?" I asked.

"I don't know," Morten said. "I mean, a drug overdose is fast. I'll call the station and get everybody working on finding her, but I'm not even sure they'll be able to in this short time."

I looked up at him. "We alert the media," I said. "That's what he wants. He wants everyone to talk about this problem, so we go out and tell it."

"How is that supposed to help find the girl?"

"I don't know, but it is. I'll call the TV station right away. And the radio. We haven't tried them yet. We ask the people to help us.

See those pill bottles? We can't see the labels, but something is wrong in this picture. No one has this many pill bottles at the same time. They're all prescription medicine. This is a person who has access to pills somehow...either the killer or the victim."

"Maybe a pharmacist?"

"Worth a try. We have to show the picture to the world. There's no time to waste."

"We can't show this picture on TV," Morten said. "People will choke on their coffee."

"We have to. Someone might recognize the girl," I said. "We have no choice."

34

FEBRUARY 2014

Anders Samuelsen felt so *alive*! He was walking around in his old house restlessly, wondering what to do next. He simply couldn't understand how he had been able to live his life behind these walls for this many years afraid of what was on the outside. There was a new voice in his head, a new and fresh voice finally telling him the truth.

You were like a living dead person in this prison. How much time you've wasted! It's time to take it all back.

And Anders was ready for it. He wanted to do everything. He wanted to see the world. He wanted to jump off every building and bridge. He wanted to live his life to the max, never letting fear hold him back again. There was no reason to. Life was fun and death even better. This was it. This was his life. He had come back for a reason. But he couldn't help but wonder what that reason was. If there was a higher purpose, then it would surely be revealed to him sooner or later, wouldn't it?

All the adrenalin rush and newfound joy about life had made it difficult for him to fall asleep at night or even to relax when he was at home. He turned on the TV, hoping it would help him calm down a little, and that was when he saw her.

The beautiful angel who had saved his life. Emma Frost. He turned up the volume and heard her angelic voice tell about how she had received an e-mail just a little while ago telling about this woman who was in danger.

"We need to save her and we need the public to help us," Emma Frost stated.

She needs me. Emma needs my help! Was that why you sent me back here, God? Was it to help her?

"We have no idea who she is or where she is and we don't have much time. The killer has given her an overdose of pills and alcohol and it will kill her within a few hours if we don't find her and get her to the hospital. We're asking for anyone who can recognize anything in this picture to please contact us. Do you know this girl?" she asked, and held up a picture so revolting it made Anders' stomach turn. A face smeared with blood, bruised beyond recognition.

"Any information about this girl or anything else in the picture can be called in to the police station," Emma Frost said. "It will be highly appreciated."

"And you have a theory as to why the killer is doing what he does?" The journalist asked.

Emma nodded. "Yes. Along with the police, we've figured out that the killer apparently wants us to focus on certain problems concerning the treatment of the mentally ill. In this case, it's the increase in the cases of mentally ill people who die from an overdose every year."

"So we're talking about a killer with a noble cause here?" The journalist said. "He is fighting for the weak, the people who can't speak for themselves?"

"Yeah, well...I'm not sure I'd put it that way, exactly," Emma Frost said. "I mean he has brutally murdered two people, buried one alive and now given this young woman an overdose which might end up killing her. He's no Robin Hood if you ask me. He's more like a terrorist holding all of us captive."

"Thank you."

"You're welcome."

A phone number to the local police station appeared up on the screen just as Anders turned off the TV. He got up and started walking in circles in his living room. The voice was in his mind again.

A killer with a noble cause, huh? Is there such a thing? After all, he did help you didn't he? He made your life better, didn't he? He made you face your fears? He helped you conquer them! He's the true hero here. He's the one who saved you. Not her.

Anders pulled his hair and looked at himself in the mirror in the bathroom. "But Emma doesn't like what he does," he told his own reflection. "Emma saved me."

He picked up a bottle of pills from the sink and looked at it. He used to take them to keep his anxiety down. Now, he hadn't taken any for days and he felt better than ever, didn't he? He was so alive. His thoughts were so clear.

You know what you have to do, don't you? You already know what's expected of you. There are people out there that need your help. You have to join the cause.

35

APRIL 2007

"**H**E'S ALRIGHT. **H**E'S RESTING." The doctor's words relieved Alexandra when she arrived at the hospital where they had taken Samuel in an ambulance after finding him in his room at the school. It had taken them almost three hours to get there and Alexandra had imagined the worst scenarios while Poul was driving. On the ferry, she had panicked and again while crossing the bridge to go to Zeeland. Poul had managed to calm her down, but she had been surprised to realize how he seemed to take it all in stride.

She couldn't escape the thought that her husband had somehow stopped loving their son.

No, it's ridiculous. He's his father. He's just has a hard time knowing how to deal with him. That's all.

"When can we see him?" Alexandra asked. She felt her heavy stomach and hoped little Olivia hadn't sensed her stress and anxiety the last several hours. They said the baby could feel all the emotions the mother experienced. Alexandra wasn't quite sure she believed that. She hoped it wasn't true.

"Right away. He really wants to see you," the doctor said.

"And he's going to be alright?" Alexandra asked.

"Yes. He didn't take the entire bottle of painkillers, so it wasn't too bad. We pumped his stomach and he'll be fine. We got him in just in time. Tests will show if the pills did any damage to his kidneys, but I don't believe they did. Your boy will be just fine."

"Ah, that's good to hear," Alexandra sighed with a smile. She looked at Poul who still seemed troubled.

"Let's go see him," she said.

Poul nodded. "Yes. Let's go."

Samuel looked up when they entered. His eyes were red. He was crying. Alexandra couldn't hold it back any longer either. Tears rolled down her cheeks.

"Samuel," she said.

He looked at her with tear-filled eyes. "I'm so sorry, Mom."

She walked closer and stroked his hair. She had no idea what to say next. That she forgave him for stabbing her? That it was going to be alright?

"Shh. Don't talk. You need to rest now, Sammy. You need all your strength to get better."

He grabbed her arm. "Mom. I need you. I need your help. I'm so sorry. I really am. I'm so sorry. I know I'm bad. I know I'm wrong, Mommy. I can change. I know I can. I need help. I hear all these voices in my head. They tell me what to do. They told me to stab you, Mommy. They told me to take those pills. I really hate the school, Mommy. They tease me. They beat me up. I'm scared of them, Mom. Please let me come back home with you and Dad. I know I can get better. I know I can. Please give me a second chance. I love you Mom, you know I do."

Alexandra cried harder now. She leaned over and hugged her son. She looked into his eyes and stroked his cheek. Yes, that was her Sammy. There he was. She could recognize him in his gentle eyes. She had always known he was in there somewhere. Oh how she loved those eyes.

"Please, Mom," he pleaded. "Please forgive me."

Alexandra tilted her head and stroked his cheek again. She had missed him so much...her sweet Sammy. How could she turn him down? How could she let him down now that he was finally reaching out to her?

Well, she couldn't.

"Of course I forgive you, Samuel. I love you so much."

Samuel smiled behind the tears. "Does that mean I can come back home?"

Alexandra answered without consulting Poul. It just flew right out of her mouth. "Of course, sweetie. Of course you can come back home."

36

FEBRUARY 2014

"**S**OMEONE RECOGNIZED THE WOMAN!**"** Morten yelled at me with the phone still in his hand.

"Really?"

"Yes. A woman called the police station. A pharmacist. She didn't recognize the face, but when she saw the bottles, she was convinced it was her. She had just given her the pills a few hours before. She is almost a hundred percent sure it's her."

"That's great news," I exclaimed. "Wonderful. So you have a name and everything?"

"Not yet. The pharmacist had to go back to the pharmacy and log into her computer in order to find the name and address from the prescription. But it shouldn't take long."

The phone rang again and Morten took it. He wrote on a piece of paper while I took out the slightly-burnt lasagna that I had forgotten in the oven. I blew on it, then removed the burnt parts.

"Still edible," I said.

"Her name is Dagmar Madsen," Morten said. "She lives in central Nordby."

"Well, that's only like a minute from here. What are we waiting for?" I asked and grabbed my jacket from the closet in the hall.

I yelled to my dad that we were leaving for a couple of hours and that food was on the counter before we rushed out to the police car. Morten followed me and started the car. We drove through the streets of Nordby with wailing sirens and parked in front of a hair-dresser's shop. Then, we jumped out of the car and pressed all the buttons on the intercom until someone buzzed us inside. We jumped up the stairs and reached Dagmar's door. Morten knocked, explaining to me that he had to knock and declare who he was before we could break in. When no one answered, he kicked in the door and soon we were both standing in Dagmar's small apartment. We checked the bedroom, the living room and the kitchen, but found no trace of Dagmar.

"Well, it was almost too easy," I said, and sat in one of her kitchen chairs.

"I know what you mean," Morten said. "This guy isn't exactly known for making things easy on us."

"So, what do we do now?"

"I have to admit, I don't know. We'll have a search team go through the apartment and hope they come up with something, but it might take a while."

"And we don't even have a little while," I said with a sigh.

I threw a glance around the apartment, with the hope that I'd find something. After all, the killer had given me a clue the last time, so there had to be something here to help me out, didn't there?

I was relieved to realize that I was right.

On the counter, I spotted a picture that caught my attention. "What's that?" I asked and got up.

"What's what?"

I grabbed the picture and looked at it.

"What is it?" Morten asked.

I showed it to him.

"What's that? A cat?"

"It looks like it."

"So what does that mean?"

"Look around. Dagmar doesn't have a cat. There is no tray in the bathroom. No bowl of food in the kitchen. Not a single cat hair in the entire apartment."

"Okay, Sherlock. Where are you going with this?"

"The picture isn't Dagmar's. Someone placed the photograph here for us to find."

37

FEBRUARY 2014

"A CAT?"

Morten looked confused. "What is that supposed to mean?"

"I don't know," I said, still staring at the picture in my hand.

"Cat, cat, cat. Maybe the killer likes cats? Maybe this is his?"

"Hm, not likely," I said. "He would never leave a hint that leads us to him. He's not the one we need to find. It's her. He doesn't want to get caught."

"True. He's way too clever to leave any clues about himself. But what else do we have?"

"It's a clue that is supposed to guide us to where Dagmar is being hidden, so it might have something to do with a place of some sort. A pet shop maybe?"

Morten cleared his throat. "It's a possibility."

"We don't have the time to take chances. One wrong move and Dagmar is gone. We'll be too late."

"Tell me about it. So what else could it be?" Morten asked.

I shook my head. My brain felt so exhausted. "I don't know. I mean what the heck is this? A yellow cat? What could that hint mean?"

"A yellow cat? Did you say yellow cat?"

"Yeah. You saw the picture. It's yellow, or maybe light orange, I don't know what they call it. I'm more of a dog person."

"The Yellow Cat is a place outside of town," Morten said. "A small inn that opened a couple of years ago. I know the owner."

I opened my eyes wide. "Let's go check it out."

Morten followed me back down to the car. We drove out of town on the slippery roads while Morten called the station and told them where we were going.

"The forensics team from Copenhagen is on their way to Dagmar's apartment and will have it searched for fingerprints and so on. I'm so happy we still had them on the island so we don't have to wait."

Morten drove out into the countryside where the streetlights stopped and there was a long distance between farms.

"Why would our killer bring Dagmar all the way out here?" I asked, while snowflakes started dancing in front of the headlights.

Just perfect. It's snowing again.

"Who knows?" Morten said. "To play with us? Make us work for it? I don't know and I don't think I really care as long as we find her...alive."

"But most of what he does seems to have a meaning of some sort. Like when he placed the head of a mentally ill person on the body of a social worker. I mean, becoming mentally ill could happen to anybody...even a social worker. Maybe by giving her the head of the mentally ill person, she would be able to better understand them. It's still a theory, but I think I'm on to something. It all has a meaning."

"Not all of it. What about the cemetery?" Morten asked.

"I've been thinking a lot about that. I believe he wanted to show us something by burying Anders Samuelsen."

"Like what?"

"Don't laugh. But I believe he wanted somehow to describe to us what it feels like to be like Anders Samuelsen. He was trapped in his house because of his fear and anxiety. He was unable to live his life properly. Like he was buried alive, like a living dead person."

Morten scoffed. "You're overanalyzing him, I think. He chose the cemetery because it's creepy and scary...that's why. He's nothing but a simple killer."

"I wouldn't call him simple," I said. "What he does demands a certain amount of intelligence."

"You sound like you're fascinated," Morten asked, skeptically.

"I'm not. I'm not going to give him that pleasure. But, I'm just saying that we're up against someone really clever and I think it's going to be really difficult to catch him."

Morten drove over a hill and stopped the car in front of an old building with a sign outside.

The Yellow Cat.

"It looks closed," I said, when we got out of the car.

"That's what worries me. It's not that late. I tried to call from the car, but no one answered the phone. It got me thinking that something was really wrong, but I didn't want to worry you further as well."

I saw Morten grab his gun and pull it out. "Maybe you'd better stay outside, Emma," he said, and walked towards the front entrance.

38

FEBRUARY 2014

I watched as Morten tried to open the door to the main entrance of the inn.

He turned and looked at me. "It's locked."

"That's odd," I said.

"I have to go in," Morten said, and kicked the door open. "You stay here."

I walked back to the car with a growing knot of concern in my stomach. I didn't like this at all and wondered if I should call for back-up.

It'll take them at least twenty minutes to get here.

My heart was beating hard as I heard Morten yell something from inside the inn. I walked closer to better hear him.

"Emma. Get in here. I need your help!"

I ran inside and found Morten in the lobby of the inn. "Is it safe?" I asked.

"I think so. Come here and help me."

That was when I realized Morten was bent over something. It looked like a body. I walked closer and saw a man tied up with duct tape. I leaned over and pulled the piece from his mouth. The man screamed in pain.

"Aw!"

"Sorry."

Morten cut his hands and feet loose with his pocket knife and soon the man was sitting up.

"What happened Ole?" Morten asked.

The man wiped his mouth repeatedly with his hand. "This glue tastes disgusting," he grunted.

"You're the owner of this inn?" I asked.

Ole nodded. "Yes."

"What happened?" Morten repeated.

Ole shook his head like he was trying to remember. "I...I have no idea. I was sitting here behind the counter this afternoon, hoping that a tourist would stop by. Things have been a little slow lately for business and I haven't had a guest in...two weeks, I think. So when a car pulled up and someone entered the inn, I was certain my luck had finally turned." Ole stopped and looked pensive. "I really don't remember much after that."

"Who entered?" Morten asked. "Was it a man?"

"Yes. It was a man. He had long blond hair and was wearing a long black cotton coat. And...uh...glasses, yes that's it. Pretty thick glasses."

I looked at Morten. "Sounds like our guy from Anders Samuelsen's sketch."

"Sure does. What else do you remember? Was he alone?" Morten asked.

"Yes. I believe he was. He...he walked up to the counter and I said *Welcome! Are you here to stay for the night?* Then he...he pulled something out of his pocket. A spray of some sort. A small bottle. Before I could react, he sprayed something in my face. It smelled really bad. Then I became dizzy and I remember feeling really nauseated and...then...this blurry vision...well, that's all I remember."

Morten sniffed. "Smells like ether. He was probably using an ether-filled perfume bottle. Those have been known to be used in bank robberies."

"So, where is he now?" I asked.

Ole shrugged. "I have no idea. He can hardly have stolen anything from me, since I don't have much money in the cash register and nothing of real value here."

"I'll run a check," Morten said. He pulled out his gun and started walking around the inn. I stayed with Ole. He looked pale.

"Can I get you anything? A glass of water?" I asked.

"Yes. Please. That would be very nice. I still feel really nauseated. There's a water cooler in the office behind the counter."

I walked into the office and found the water cooler and poured some in a plastic cup, while casting a glance around the room. My eyes fell on a picture of a building he had put up on the wall. I grabbed the plastic cup and walked back to Ole, who was still sitting on the floor. I kneeled next to him and handed it to him. He drank greedily.

"So, what's your relationship to Hummelgaarden?" I asked, while he drank.

He finished the cup. "That really hit the spot, thank you so much. Hummelgaarden you say?"

I nodded. "I saw a picture of it in your office."

"Well, it's a long story, but it has a special place in my heart. I used to work there."

39

JUNE 2007

Alexandra had her baby three weeks early and had to stay in the hospital for a week after the birth in order to make sure the baby was strong enough to be brought home. It was a hard time on all of them, but it especially took its toll on Poul who had to stay alone in the house with Samuel.

Alexandra was worried and found it hard to sleep at the hospital at night.

"The baby will be fine," the doctors and nurses kept telling her. "You need your sleep. You have to relax or you'll only get sick. You won't be able to produce enough milk for your baby if you don't get your rest. She is small and weak and only your milk can give her strength and make her grow. Rest is vital for both of you. Right now, your daughter needs you more than she ever will. She needs you to be well and rested."

But Alexandra wasn't worried about little Olivia. That wasn't why she stayed awake all night and wandered in circles in her room, not being able to lay still. No, she was concerned about Poul and Samuel being all alone in the house.

I just hope they don't kill each other.

Things had been turning from bad to worse to terrifying ever since she had brought Samuel home from the hospital. Poul had been so angry with her because she made the decision at the hospital without even consulting him first. It had started already on the evening when they brought him home.

"I don't want the boy living in my house again. I don't trust him, Alexandra. He tried to kill you, remember?"

"No, he didn't. It was an accident."

"It wasn't an accident, Alexandra. Don't make excuses for the boy. He stabbed you on purpose."

"I don't think he meant to harm me, Poul. I really don't. He just couldn't control himself. Besides, it won't happen again. He's changed. He regrets it so much. Didn't you see it in his eyes at the hospital? He's back. He's our sweet little Samuel again. Didn't you hear him? I mean, he is our son, for crying out loud. We have to love him. We have to care for him. We have to forgive him."

"Well, I certainly don't. I think he only said all those things because he wanted you to take him home. I'm certain he only tried to kill himself because he wanted to come home. He didn't even take enough pills to kill himself...the doctor told us so. He's just acting, Alexandra, and you're falling for it. It's all just a clever act. Can't you see that?"

"No!" Alexandra said, crying heavily and worrying that Samuel would hear every word his dad was saying from his room next door where he was supposed to be sleeping. "He's a good boy. I know he is. He's just not well. Somewhere in there is my boy and I am determined to find him. I saw him today at the hospital. The way he looked at me. There was true deep love in those eyes. He can change. He told me he would. I know he can. We'll get him the help he needs. We have to try, Poul. We have to give him a second chance."

That was when she had seen it in Poul's eyes. Pure hatred for the boy. That was when she realized that Poul blamed everything on Samuel. He thought the boy had ruined everything for them and now that he was in their lives again, he was going to destroy it all. Poul shook his head and lifted his hands. "I'm not. I won't forgive him and I refuse to let him manipulate me. I see right through that act of his. He is dangerous, Alex."

"Don't say that. It's an awful thing to say. He's your son," Alexandra hissed in anger and frustration. She couldn't believe that Poul would abandon her on this matter. They were supposed to stick together, to back each other up. Why did he refuse to see what she had seen in the boy? He was there with them in the hospital room. Didn't he see the boy crying his heart out?"

Now, while lying in the hospital bed, Alexandra was scared of what the two of them might end up doing to one another. She was terrified of the future and what they should do with the boy. Where would he go to school?

She worried about those things constantly in the hospital until one morning when they rolled in a new roommate for her. It was a woman who told her that she had a nephew who struggled with mental issues as well. Alexandra found much comfort talking to this woman during the daytime and told her about her worries and troubles at home.

"Well, my sister felt just as frustrated as you until Tommy's social worker sent him to this new place outside of town that just opened a few months ago...it's an institution of some sort, I think. Anyway, it completely changed things for him and for my sister."

"That sounds really good. Maybe I should try and get Samuel in there as well," Alexandra said, suddenly sparked with newfound hope.

"You should. Talk to a social worker at City Hall. The place is called Hummelgaarden."

40

FEBRUARY 2014

"**T**HE PLACE IS SECURE."

Morten came back just as I was about to ask Ole more about Hummelgaarden. Morten looked at me, concerned. "Unfortunately, no signs of Dagmar either."

I rose to my feet with a frustrated sigh. "But there has to be. I mean, the killer led us here."

Morten shook his head. "I'm sorry. You're welcome to check for yourself. I've been in all the rooms upstairs. It's not that big of an inn." Morten looked at Ole. "Is there anywhere else he could have hidden her?" he asked.

"There is the wine cellar," Ole said.

"I'll go check," Morten said, and disappeared.

I looked at Ole. Some of the color had returned to his cheeks. "Feeling better?" I asked.

He nodded. "I think so."

I helped him get on his feet again. "So you used to work at Hummelgaarden, huh?"

"Yes, well it's a long time ago. Now I have this place. It was always my dream to start something of my own, you know?"

I nodded, wondering if it could be a coincidence that Ole used to work there.

Morten came back upstairs and brought me out of my thought pattern. "Nope. Nothing there either," he said.

"That's strange," I said. "Why would the killer bring us here if he hasn't hidden Dagmar here?"

Morten shrugged. "I don't know. I'm getting a little tired of his games. I've called for the forensics team to come out here once they're done with Dagmar's apartment and secure any trace of the killer. Did he touch anything while he was here?"

Ole shrugged. "I...I don't know. Maybe the door handle."

I looked at Ole. "What's that?" I asked, pointing at the pocket on the chest of his shirt. It was bulging like there was something in it.

Ole felt it. "I don't know." He put his fingers inside it and pulled something out.

"What is it?" Asked Morten.

"I...I don't know," Ole said. "I don't remember ever seeing this before. It looks like a...like one of those key chains the tourists buy."

"And you say you didn't put it in your pocket?" I asked.

"I never put anything in that pocket," Ole answered.

"It's a clue," I said, looking at Morten.

He exhaled. "This guy is unbelievable!" He looked at me. "So where are we supposed to go now?"

I shrugged. "There is a key on it."

"Yeah but where does it fit?"

"Maybe we can find out if we go down to one of the shops at the harbor where they sell these things?" I asked.

Ole and Morten looked at one another. "Actually, that's not a bad idea," Morten said.

"Then let's go," I said. I looked at Ole. "Will you be alright? The place will be swamped with police in a few minutes. Should we call for an ambulance as well? Do you want the paramedics to take a look at you?"

Ole shook his head. "I'm fine, but thanks."

I smiled and nodded. "Well, thanks for your help."

"Call us if you remember anything else," Morten said. "Any little detail might help us."

"Sure."

Morten and I drove through the countryside and passed the Copenhagen forensic team in their blue vans going the other direction on our way back to town. My heart was still pumping hard in my chest. I was worried about Dagmar. This little trip to the inn had taken a long time. My hopes that she would survive were decreasing by the second.

Morten parked the car in the middle of the street downtown and we jumped out.

Morten stopped. He looked at me.

"There are three souvenir shops on this street. Which one do we pick?"

I scanned the many small souvenir shops. They all looked alike. Except for one. I pointed at it.

"We pick the one where the light is turned on inside. Come on."

41

FEBRUARY 2014

Anders Samuelsen was getting ready. He looked at himself in the mirror and lifted his head in pride. It was the first time he was wearing the Shinobi Shozoko, the traditional ninja uniform, since he bought it online five years ago. Until now, it had been hanging on the wall in his bedroom next to the Katana, the Japanese sword that he was now taking down for the first time in years as well. He pulled it carefully out of its scabbard and looked at it. It was long and slim, but very, very sharp. He touched it gently with his finger and cut a little skin off.

"Perfect," he said from underneath the black uniform that was covering his mouth. Actually, it was covering all of his body except for a small slit around his eyes and hands.

Anders looked down at his Tabi boots with the slit between the big toe and the second toe.

"Made to make it easier to climb ropes and scale walls," he said satisfied, while studying them. It was truly a remarkable outfit. Perfect for his purpose.

Anders had studied ninjas for years and years from his computer while being imprisoned by his fears, dreaming about one day becoming as forceful and ferocious as them. For years he had admired these soldiers, but never dared to become one himself. Now the time had come for him to get out of his shell. For years, he had been hiding like a coward in this house, hiding from his true purpose and destiny.

Anders stood in front of the mirror in the hallway holding his sword up in front of him, then he pretended to be using it in a fight. He killed the imaginary enemy, then smiled at his own reflection.

"Brilliant," he said. "Simply brilliant."

For years, the fear and medicine had held Anders back. Now it was time for him to shine. He was no longer afraid of anything. He had faced his worst fears and so should the rest of the world. No one in this world should ever have to be afraid again.

Anders was going to make sure of that.

He opened the front door and walked out into the snow, not letting the cold get to him, even if it was biting at his fingers.

Silent and secretively, he rushed into the black night, disappearing like the wind. He ran across the street, found a sidewalk, ran up the hill and down towards town.

He was panting heavily and his knees were freezing when he reached center of town. He wasn't in as good of shape as he would like to be. He passed several small houses and looked in the windows, where people were sitting in their cozy living rooms, watching TV or sitting around the dinning table and chatting. Anders stared at them, then moved on. He was looking for the right person. He ran towards another house and looked inside. He spotted a woman sitting in a chair in front of the TV. She seemed to be alone.

"Perfect," Anders mumbled, staying in position for ten minutes more to make sure she really was alone. When no other person showed up in the room, Anders assumed she was, in fact, all alone, and got himself ready to make his move. He took in a deep breath and closed his eyes to reach a state of complete calmness. Then he pulled out the sword from the scabbard attached to his back, ran towards the front door and gave it a kick to make it jump open. With a high-pitched scream he sprang inside the house and ran to the living room, making all the sounds he had heard ninjas make in the many movies he had watched.

The woman in the chair screamed with fear. Anders swung the sword in the air, then yelled:

"Fear not, lady. Never fear again. I'm here to free you from your fears and anxiety. They're holding you back! They're the ones keeping you from living your life. I will make you free. I am *the Deliverer!*"

The woman didn't seem to listen much to his words. She still stared at him with deep anxiety in her eyes and screamed at the top of her lungs. Anders knew exactly how she felt at that moment. He himself had felt it down in that coffin buried underground. It was the certainty that this was her last moment alive; it was knowing that this was it.

She was exactly in the place Anders wanted her to be in. It was perfect. Now, all he had to do was to show her that there was absolutely no reason to fear death. It was nothing to be afraid of. But the only way she could really fully understand that, was if she actually died and came back. Just like he had.

He wanted her to experience the peace he had felt and he wanted her to come back and look at the world with the same newfound courage and wonder that he had.

"Please don't hurt me," she pleaded. "Please don't."

Anders tilted his head and looked at her. Then he swung the sword towards her with the words:

"I'm sorry. But this is a necessary part of the process. You will thank mc later."

Anders pierced sword into the woman's stomach and blood started gushing out. Then he pulled the sword back out again. She stared at him with wide open eyes. With her hand, she felt the blood.

Anders saw how life slowly oozed out of her eyes, as they rolled back in her head and she fell out of the chair and onto the ground. Then he smiled, picked up her phone holding it with a small handkerchief he had brought with him.

"I need an ambulance to Valdemarsvej. Yes its number 43. It's serious, yes, very. A woman has been stabbed. You need to hurry."

Then he hung up, turned on his heel and looked at the woman whose lifeless body was crumbling on the floor. He couldn't stop smiling. He walked closer, then bowed elegantly.

"You're very welcome."

42

FEBRUARY 2014

Morten walked in front of me with his gun held up. We reached the front door of the shop and he pulled the handle.

"It's open," he whispered. "You better stand back. If the killer is in there, he might be armed."

"Sure," I said, stopping while Morten continued inside. I heard him gasp.

"Morten?"

"I'm alright."

"Can I come in?"

"I don't know if it's such a good idea," Morten said. "It's pretty bad in here. Call for an ambulance will you?"

I fumbled to find my phone then called the alarm central. "They say the island's only ambulance is already on its way to another incident in town. Is it a life-threatening situation?"

Morten groaned. "I guess not. I'm pretty sure she's already dead."

My heart stopped. "Is it Dagmar?"

"No. This one is much older."

I didn't care what Morten had said, I walked inside the shop with the phone still to my ear. Then I gasped as well. Morten was standing in the middle of the room next to the body of a woman who had been strung up by her legs, hanging upside down, the head, decapitated, lying on the floor beneath her.

I felt nauseated and covered my eyes. "She's definitely dead. Just send an ambulance when you can," I said and hung up.

"She's been dead for a long time," Morten said. "There is no blood anywhere."

"Who is she?" I asked, when I dared to look again and removed my hand. "I mean was?"

"Her name is Marianne Moeller," Morten said. "She owns the shop. I've been down here on more than one occasion when she called for us to help throw out troublesome Eastern European tourists that she caught stealing."

I shook my head in disbelief. "I don't understand. Why did she have to die?"

"Still looking for meaning to it all?" Morten asked.

I shrugged. Then I heard a sound. "What was that?" I asked.

Morten pulled his gun again.

"Sounds like it came from that closet right there," I said and pointed and an old wooden armoire leaning against the wall.

"Stand back," Morten said and tried to pull it open. "It's locked."

I put a hand in my pocket and pulled out the keychain that Ole had in his shirt pocket.

"Maybe this will fit?"

"Try it."

My hands were shaking while I put the key in the hole and turned it. As I opened the closet, a body fell out and landed on the floor with a thud. I screamed and looked down at it.

It was Dagmar.

There was no doubt. I recognized her from the picture. Morten bent down and felt for a pulse.

"She's still alive. Heavily sedated, but alive."

I kneeled next to her. "Dagmar? Can you hear us?" I looked up at Morten. "We need to get this stuff out of her. Would you help me?"

Morten nodded.

"Grab her body and help her up."

Morten helped me get her to stand upright. "She's heavy."

"I know, but just hold her for a few minutes."

Dagmar moaned.

"What are you planning on doing?"

"It's gonna take a while for the ambulance to get here and be able to pump her stomach. We need to get those pills out now. I have to make her throw up."

I had tried this once before with Maya when she was younger and had swallowed a pack of my birth control pills, thinking they were candy. So, just like the last time, I simply stuck a finger down the woman's throat and let it stay until she started gagging. A few seconds later, she threw up all over the floor.

43

FEBRUARY 2014

That night, Morten and I both had trouble sleeping. He was tossing and turning, while I was mostly staring at the ceiling where the moonlight from outside lit it up. It had cleared up and finally stopped snowing and the full moon was shining brightly outside, making it even harder for me to sleep with all the light.

I kept thinking about Dagmar and Marianne Moeller in the shop. I was happy that we had been able to save Dagmar, but sad that Marianne had to die. It was terrible. Furthermore, the paramedics told me that there had been another murder attempt downtown on the same night. A woman had been stabbed in her own living room and they weren't sure she would survive.

What the heck was going on in this town? Was the killer just killing randomly now? Where was the silver lining in all these killings? Maybe there wasn't any. Maybe he was just crazy; maybe he was just mentally ill.

Oh my God, Victor. What am I supposed to do about Victor?

Well, I guess I had to see if we could get a social worker from City Hall to take care of our case. I had no idea where else to turn.

The situation wasn't sustainable for him right now. He was allowed in school, but they wanted me to find another solution as soon as possible.

I managed to finally fall asleep an hour before the alarm clock sounded, then tumbled out of bed and walked downstairs to prepare breakfast. My dad was sitting in the kitchen when I walked in. I had completely forgotten about him.

"Good morning, sweetie," he said, looking up from his paper.

"Dad? You're still here?" I asked, worried that he would run into my mother again. Then I wondered where she was, if she had even come home last night after her date.

"Yes. When you didn't come back and it was after midnight, I took one of the guestrooms."

"Of course," I said. "I had completely forgotten you were here. Thank you so much for being in the house with the kids while I was gone."

"No problem, sweetheart. You know how much I enjoy spending time with those munchkins."

I laughed and kissed his forehead. "Yes, I know. But thanks anyway." I found some sliced bread and toasted it. Then I poured some cereal in a bowl for Victor. "So Mom didn't come home before midnight either, huh?"

My dad looked down at his paper. His eyes avoided mine when he spoke. "No. I guess she didn't."

I found orange juice, cheese, and butter in the refrigerator and put them on the table. I put a piece of bread on a plate and handed it to my dad. "Here."

"You sure you don't want me to leave right away?" he asked. "It could get awkward."

"I know, but you were here first. As a matter of fact, you're the only one who has always been here for us. So, at least let me treat you to a decent breakfast. Only leave if you're uncomfortable with the situation. I'll make some coffee."

"Thanks, sweetie. I don't want to cause any trouble, you know."

"I do know. But you're not the one causing trouble, if you know what I mean," I said, as I poured water in the coffeemaker.

My dad smiled, then continued to read the paper. I looked at the front cover, then stopped.

"What the...?" I leaned over and grabbed the paper out of my dad's hand.

"What are you doing?"

"What's this?" I asked, pointing at the front cover.

My dad shrugged.

"You've got to be kidding me! *The Caring Killer?*"

"That's what they call him, yes. They think he cares about the mentally ill or something. He kills with a purpose, they say. Almost makes him a hero, doesn't it? There is an article in here about how he helped save Hummelgaarden and how he now wants us all to focus on drugs for the mentally ill. How the drugs are not controlled and, therefore, many die because they can't control it themselves. The paper is filled with stories like this. They found lots of family members to tell their stories. It's actually filling the entire paper. There's a nice portrait of Hummelgaarden as well, telling about all they have accomplished up there...how many kids they've helped. Like this guy for instance," my dad said and took the paper from my hands. He flipped a couple of pages and showed me the picture of a young boy.

"This boy kept getting himself in trouble because he was so aggressive. Ever since he moved to Hummelgaarden, his grades have improved and he is no longer fighting everybody."

"Well, that's great, but still...come on, the man kills people to get his message out. Calling him something as stupid as The Caring Killer and making a hero out of him is really bad."

"They don't actually make a hero out of him. They just tell people that there is a purpose to what he is doing, even if it is horrible."

"But that's exactly what he wants. They're just doing precisely what he wants them to do. If he can get his message out like this, then who knows who else will follow him and try to do something similar? There are plenty of lunatics out there."

44

FEBRUARY 2014

I felt frustrated and angry most of the day. It was such an annoying feeling to be played with the way The Caring Killer was playing me and everyone else on the island. Even the media from the mainland had caught interest in the story now and it was all over. They were calling me like crazy asking me to tell everything I knew about The Caring Killer and why I thought he had chosen me. I refused to talk to any of them. I simply couldn't be a part of all this, of this grand plan of his. I felt like a puppet.

My mother hadn't shown her face all day and I was beginning to wonder if she had even come home at all. I tried not to care. At least I had a great morning with my dad and didn't have to worry about her coming down and ruining everything. I thought about going to her room several times to see if she was up there, but decided not to. It was none of my business what she did with her life.

Morten called me in the afternoon, just before the kids returned from school. I was happy to hear his voice, but hated the fact that all we ever talked about these days was the killer and the case. I wanted Morten to catch him as quickly as possible so I could get back to my life again, but, as it turned out, it wasn't so easy. I didn't even dare to turn on my computer for fear of what might wait for me next. I was certain The Caring Killer wasn't done yet.

"So, what's new?" I asked Morten.

"Busy morning. I thought you'd like to know that Dagmar is going to be fine. We went to the mainland to visit her this morning and interview her and the doctor told us it didn't look like any of her internal organs had suffered any damage. They were going to keep her for a week and run more tests just to be sure, but so far it seems like you've saved her."

"Well, you were there as well," I said, thinking it was so sweet of him to try and comfort me by telling me this. "I wasn't alone."

"I know. But you really did well yesterday. Making her throw up saved her life, they told me. I can't believe you did that."

"I guess my motherly instincts took over," I chuckled. "It really wasn't so bad."

"Pretty brave if you ask me," Morten said. "Should have been you on the front cover of that paper this morning instead. You're the hero here."

"Thanks, that's really sweet of you to say."

"I mean it." He paused.

"So what did Dagmar tell you? Did she see his face?"

"She can't remember anything. Apparently, one of the pills she was forced to take causes amnesia, so she doesn't remember one damn thing. All she remembers is buying the pills at the pharmacy and coming home with them. Everything after that is completely blacked out."

"Oh no. That's awful."

"What about the other woman? The one who was attacked in her living room?" I asked.

"It's the strangest thing. She's going to be fine too. She was lucky, the doctor said, but the stab didn't hit anything vital. She lost a lot of blood, but will survive. She was actually able to talk to us when we were in the hospital to talk to Dagmar."

"Did she see his face?"

"That's the strange part about it. She told us she was watching TV when, suddenly, the door to her house was kicked in and...get this...a ninja jumped inside her living room and tried to kill her with his ninja-sword. She told us he was dressed exactly like a ninja, all in black and it covered his face. She could see his eyes, though, so we'll have a sketcher make a drawing of them."

"Doesn't exactly match with the man with heavy glasses that we had on the first sketch," I said.

"Unless he was wearing the glasses as a disguise."

"True."

"The strangest part of what she told me was what The Caring Killer said to her before he stabbed her."

"Don't call him that. It's catching on," I said.

"I'm sorry. I can't help it. Everyone down here calls him that. It's horrible. I know," he said apologetically.

"I know. I do it myself. So what did he say to her?"

"He called himself The Deliverer. He told her he was going to *set her free from her fears.*"

"What?" I asked. This was getting more and more strange.

"I know. It sounds raving mad, doesn't it? He's a pure lunatic if you ask me," Morten said.

"I don't know about that," I said.

"What do you mean?"

"It doesn't sound like him."

"Why not?" Morten asked, surprised. "It sounds exactly like him if you ask me. He has a purpose, remember? He wanted to set her free of her fears."

"Yeah, but his purpose was different before. It was to have us focus on things that weren't right. This seems somehow much different."

"It sounds exactly the same to me," Morten said. I could sense a slight annoyance in his voice. He really wanted it to be our killer. He wanted him to be raving mad, but I didn't think he was. The

Caring Killer was smart, intelligent and had everything planned thoroughly.

"There is also the matter of the sword," Morten continued. "It could easily be the one used to decapitate our two social workers."

"Two?"

"Yes. It turns out Marianne Moeller from the souvenir shop used to be a social worker as well. She retired two years ago and opened her own shop downtown. According to her neighbors, she was making a lifelong dream come true."

"That makes sense," I said. "She wasn't a random victim. It was deliberate."

"Could be. It turns out, she's been dead for two weeks. Everybody thought she was on vacation. She was supposed to go to Greece and had told everybody she would be gone and the shop was closed. She loved to travel and has no family, so no one wondered where she was. Get this. It was her blood we found on Tine Solvang's face. We ran a test and it matched."

"The other social worker? So he kept them in the same freezer, did he?"

"Looks like it."

I felt nauseated again. This entire case did that to me. It was frustrating. I wondered who had a freezer big enough to fit two women's bodies. I shook my head and tried to get rid of the thought. It was no use.

"So are we still on for tonight?" Morten asked.

"What?"

"Don't tell me you forgot?"

"Uh...I didn't forget?"

"You forgot what day it is today."

I tried hard to remember.

"I got nothing."

"It's Valentine's day."

"Valentine's day. I was just about to say that. Of course I didn't forget. We were supposed to go out. It's no problem. I'll ask my mom to look after the kids," I said and looked at the door like I expected her to walk through any minute now.

As soon as I find out where she is.

"Great. I'll pick you up at six. I've made reservations."

"See you then."

45

JULY 2007

A lexandra had to bring baby Olivia with her to the meeting with the social worker at City Hall. She was waiting in the office when a woman in her mid-fifties entered. She looked at Alexandra with a grunt, then forced a smile.

"Alexandra Holm?" she asked, sitting behind her desk.

"Yes," Alexandra said.

"Marianne Moeller," the woman said. "I've been appointed as your social worker." She opened a file and flipped a few pages. "Your son, Samuel tried to kill himself recently?"

She looked at Alexandra over her glasses. The look in her eyes made Alexandra feel uncomfortable.

"Yes. He...he's had a lot of problems...uh...We've tried many things, medicine, therapy, and have seen every specialist we could, but each one gave him a different diagnosis and nothing ever helped. He's a very sensitive boy who can, at times, get very aggressive."

The social worker was nodding while looking down at the papers. "And he was at a boarding school when it happened?"

"Yes. We thought it would be good for him to have some discipline so..."

"After he had been homeschooled for years?" Marianne Moeller asked.

Alexandra didn't care much for the tone of her voice. It was condescending.

"Yes. He was expelled from school...I tried to homeschool him but couldn't..." Alexandra was about to cry. She hated to have to admit to people that she couldn't handle her own boy. "Well, to be honest, I couldn't control him."

"And you didn't think it was kind of a drastic move to suddenly put the boy in a boarding school far away from home, a home that had been his all his life up until then?"

"Well...yes, but...what I'm saying is, we couldn't...I couldn't...he was so aggressive and I...We had nowhere else to go with him. No other school would take him. What should we have done?"

The social worker shrugged. "What should you have done? Well, what do you think other parents do with their children? They discipline them, they raise them, and they punish them when they misbehave. Having an aggressive boy is not that unusual. Plus, maybe you should have looked a little into why the boy was being this aggressive, don't you think? See a family therapist. Not always focus on Samuel as being the problem. When a boy acts out in school, it is my experience that it is most often because things aren't well at home. Do your husband and you fight a lot?"

Alexandra shook her head, perplexed. "No. I mean it has taken a toll on our marriage to care for Samuel, but I hardly think..."

"Does your husband care about the boy?" Marianne Moeller asked.

Alexandra stared at her with wide open eyes. She had never felt so humiliated. "I don't see what that has to do with..."

"Does he love him? Does he hug and kiss him and tell him how wonderful he is? Do his eyes light up when he looks at him?"

"Well no, but that's..."

The social worker nodded. "More often than not, the problem is with the relationship with the father. Maybe you should work on that. And maybe you should consider that fact that Samuel might have tried to commit suicide because you and your husband suddenly decided to remove him from everything he knew and loved, placed him far away and decided to start a new family without him. Am I wrong?"

Alexandra felt the anger rise in her. She considered getting up and leaving, but she couldn't. She needed this woman's help badly.

"I don't..."

"And now you want the county to take care of him, right?" the social worker interrupted her. "Like so many other parents, you screwed up and you want us to fix it, to take the boy."

"I just heard about Hummelgaarden and heard that they do amazing things for children with mental illness. I just thought that maybe it could help him to go there. Help all of us. I have the baby to look after, as well. I simply don't have..."

"The energy to take care of a boy who needs extra attention; boy, have I heard that said in this office...many times." Marianne Moeller sighed. "The thing is, Hummelgaarden is very popular. It's fully booked for months. There's a waiting list. I could put you on that list, but to tell you the truth, your boy isn't exactly material for Hummelgaarden. Right now, we rush in patients who are being appointed here by the court. He hasn't committed any crime. So, he will most likely be overlooked, even if he gets to the top of the waiting list."

"So, you're telling me if he went out and stole a car, then he could get in?"

Marianne Moeller shrugged. "I'm not allowed to say that, but yes, that would be a reason for me to push this thing forward."

Alexandra scoffed. "That's ridiculous. The boy is dangerous. He has threatened me on several occasions. Doesn't that count for anything?"

"Not if it hasn't been reported and if he hasn't been convicted of anything. No. I need the court's word that he is dangerous."

Alexandra couldn't believe what she was hearing. It simply couldn't be true. She shook her head and looked angrily at the woman in front of her.

"Well, maybe we don't have to wait all that long. Maybe he'll kill someone and then I guess the door will be open, huh?" Alexandra snorted and got up from her chair.

Marianne Moeller took off her glasses and rubbed her forehead. "Listen. There might be something I can do for you."

Alexandra sat down again. She threw a glance at Olivia who was still sleeping in her carrycot. She was such a good sleeper. It still amazed Alexandra how calm she always was. Even when awake. She was such a joy.

"Like what?" she asked.

"Well they have a program for people like you. We can appoint Samuel to three appointments at Hummelgaarden. Three days where he can go there and stay all day and talk to one of our counselors. But that is all he can get. It's all I have."

Alexandra nodded. "I'll take it."

46

FEBRUARY 2014

I finally decided to go and check in my mother's room and ask her if she could take care of Victor tonight. I thought about letting Maya babysit, but was pretty sure she had told me on another occasion that she had made plans with her best friend for tonight.

I knocked gently on the door. "Mom?"

No one answered. I knocked again. Slightly louder this time. "Mom? Are you in there?"

"Good morning, sweetie," a voice said behind me.

Startled, I turned and looked into my mother's face. She was wearing nothing but a towel around her waist.

"I was just taking a shower," she said. She walked past me and into the room. I followed her inside.

"Did you sleep until now? It's two in the afternoon."

She shrugged. "Well, I was out a little late last night. I thought I'd sleep in. Then, I spent some time in bed chatting with Arne on Facebook."

I closed my eyes and growled. I don't know what it was. I probably just didn't enjoy watching my mother act like a teenager.

"Did you sleep with him?" I asked.

My mother looked at me. She was smiling, but her eyes told me she was insulted. "Emma!"

"I'm sorry. It's none of my business."

"Damn right, it's not."

"It just takes a little getting used to, all this, you and this sleeping in and dating the mailman, hurting Dad and all. It's getting on my nerves," I said.

My mother dropped her towel and started to get dressed in front of me. I couldn't stop staring at her. Her body looked like she was in her thirties.

"Wow, Mom. How much work did you have done?"

"I looked great, don't I?" she asked and showed off her body to me as if she was showing me a new dress. "These are new," she said and cupped both of her breasts in her hands. "Nice, right? I like how round and voluptuous they are. Don't you?"

"I...I...I don't know what to say." The truth was, they looked nicer than mine, but they still had that fake look to them. It was weird that a sixty-nine-year-old woman would have a body like that. It was simply strange. Especially since she was my mother and had never looked like this my entire childhood.

"He also removed a lot of skin from above the knees and under the arms. And sucked out all the fat from my behind," she said and turned so I could better see.

I had no idea what to say. I knew what I really thought. I knew what I wanted to say to her.

Please, stop it mom. Please just be a mother and grandmother. Please look like one. I miss you. I miss the mother I grew up with.

"Well, it looks very nice," I said instead.

She looked so happy. "Arne thought so too."

I closed my eyes. "You've got to be kidding me. You did sleep with him."

"Well, yes. Now, there you have it. Two people in the prime of their life enjoying each other. Is that so bad, huh?"

I looked at her. Then I smiled. "I guess not. As long as he doesn't hurt you Mom. As long as you're happy."

"Oh, but I am. I'm very happy indeed. He was a true gentleman, if you must know. Took me back to his place outside of town and put on some music, then asked me to dance with him. I think we danced for hours. He is such a sweet man, Emma. You won't believe it."

"Wow. Sounds like you really like him," I said, a little startled.

"I enjoy his company. As I said, he is quite the gentleman."

A gentleman who sleeps with a girl on the first date!

"We're going out tonight again."

"You are?" I asked.

"Yes. He's picking me up here at six."

"Okay. I'll have Dad look after Victor then."

"You're going out tonight?" she asked. "Morten is taking you out?"

"Yes. He's made reservations."

"Good for you. He seems to be a nice guy."

My mom was almost dressed now. She put on a red sweater. It looked great on her. I suddenly felt happy. It was good to talk to her about these things. I had missed that.

"He is very nice. Say, do me a favor, will you?"

"Sure, what?"

"Be out of here before Dad comes. I can't stand to see the hurt in his eyes. It was brutal last night."

My mother nodded pensively. "I know. I saw it too. You think he's alright?"

I was glad to hear that she cared. "He'll be fine. He still misses you, you know? It's been hard for him to get over you."

"You think he's over me now?"

I bit my lip. I had no idea how to answer that. No, he was not over my mother. Definitely not. But did he want her to know that? Did he want me to tell her he was?

"Maybe you should ask him himself one of these days," I said and walked towards the door. I turned before I walked out and looked at her. "I think it would do the both of you a lot of good if you sat down and spoke to one another. But, that's just my opinion."

I closed the door before she could protest and walked downstairs.

47

FEBRUARY 2014

Anders Samuelsen felt happy. He was sitting in his house reading in the newspaper about the woman he had visited the night before. She had survived, just like he had planned she would. He felt good about himself. Better than he ever had. Not only had he recently beat death and been freed from all of his anxiety and fears, now he was also passing this gift on to others.

What could be more fulfilling?

The newspaper stated that the police believed it was the man they called The Caring Killer who had tried to stab the woman and that suited Anders perfectly. No one would ever suspect him and that way he could go around doing his good deeds without anyone stopping him.

His ways were untraditional. He knew that, but he also knew that they would end up thanking him. That was how he felt towards The Caring Killer. He wanted so badly to thank him for saving him. Somehow, he felt that he had done that, now that he was passing this on. He was showing his gratitude. Even the new voice in his mind told him so.

That's the way it is in life. If you've been given something, you should pass it on to others. Pay it forward like that movie with that kid you like so much. It's only fair. Maybe you'll end up creating a movement, a legacy.

Anders went into the bathroom and washed the sword gently to get rid of the woman's blood. He looked at the bottles of pills on the shelf and remembered the doctor's words when he had given them to him.

"Remember to take them every day. If you cheat, if you skip just a day you might end up getting hallucinations. Maybe even a psychosis. You might lose contact with reality. It's very serious, Anders."

Anders laughed at his own reflection.

Stupid doctors. Think they're God, don't they?

The fact was, Anders didn't need the medicine. He had never felt better in his life. He was doing good for others. That was his drug now.

Anders looked at the clean sword and lifted it in the air. Then he laughed again. Tonight was Valentine's night. Everybody would be out on dates and eating romantic dinners. Meanwhile, some people would be home alone wrapped in their own fears. Like he had been on every Valentine's night he could remember. They would be lonely, afraid of going out. Those were the ones he needed to rescue. Those were the ones Anders would have to give the gift to.

The gift of life.

Maybe he was the one who was God? Only God could, after all, give the gift of life. And that was what he was doing. He was bringing these people back from death. It was truly extraordinary, wasn't it? Only God could have given him such an important task. Yes, that had to be it. God had told him to do this. He had sent the voice to help him.

Don't take this lightly, Anders. This is a very important task that only you can fulfill.

Anders put on his uniform and put the sword into his scabbard, which he attached to his back. He looked at himself in the mirror with great pride. Never had he felt this important. Never had he felt such honor.

Anders waited in his house until darkness came, then stormed into the black night, letting the darkness swallow him.

He ran till he came to a small street with many houses. He found a house and walked up to the window to look into it. Inside, he spotted a woman. She seemed to be alone. The room was packed with toys on the floor. Soon, the door to the living room opened and a kid came in, followed by another and another. They were all in pajamas. Anders counted their heads. There were five of them in total.

48

FEBRUARY 2014

"Your mom is out with him again? I don't like the guy."

"Well big surprise, Dad. You don't like the guy Mom is dating."

He chuckled. "Okay, I guess you're right. I am slightly biased."

I laughed at my dad. He had arrived at the house to take care of Victor while the rest of us had a night out. My mom had taken my advice and asked Arne to come half an hour earlier, so they had already left when my dad came. Maya was going out with her best friend. They were apparently meeting up with two boys from school who had invited them out on a double date. Meanwhile, I had put on a nice dress and slapped some make-up on my face to help me look decent. I hated getting all dressed up, but apparently Morten enjoyed it because he was one big smile as he entered the house.

"Wow. Emma. You look...You're stunning," he said in the sweetest trembling voice.

I blushed. "Thank you."

"Shall we?" he asked and held out his hand.

"Let's. Dad, the food is on the stove. Victor is in his room reading gross books about the French Revolution. Call me if there is anything, okay?"

"Yeah, yeah. Everything is fine. I've got it. As usual. Go have fun. Eat a steak for me. Be romantic for all of us lonely people."

"We will," Morten said and dragged me out of the house.

I got in his car and we drove off.

"What's wrong?" Morten asked. "You're very quiet all of a sudden."

I shook my head. "It's nothing. It's just my dad. His last remark hit me hard. I hate that he has to be alone on a night like this."

"I know what you mean. I saw that look in his eyes." Morten put his hand on my shoulder. "But don't let it ruin our night. You can't do anything about it anyway."

I sniffled. "I know. I just hate to see him like this. All heart-broken and mushy. It's so unlike him. Meanwhile, my mom is out having the time of her life with my mailman."

"All children want their parents to be together. That's only natural. But it's out of your hands. They're grown-ups. You can't fix their problems."

I exhaled and leaned my head back in the seat. "You're right."

"I'm what? Could you say that again? Don't think I heard it?"

I laughed and batted at him, gently. I put my head on his shoulder. "I love you," I said.

My heart stopped. I hadn't told him that before. Neither of us had ever said it to the other. I wanted to do it on the right occasion. Now, I had just blurted it out. He wasn't one to use big words like that. He picked his words carefully. That was why I had held back. I was afraid of scaring him away. I looked up at his face. He didn't seem disturbed or surprised in any way.

"I love you too," he said.

I smiled and put my head back on his shoulder. "That's established then."

Morten pulled the car over to the side of the road and parked in front of a building. I peeked out the window and read the sign.

"Restaurant Cornelius?" I looked at him. "That's way too expensive for you."

"Well, I know I don't make as much as you, but I wanted to treat you today."

"Are you sure? 'Cause I would be just as happy in a smaller, less-pricey place downtown?"

I felt his hand in my lap. "Let me do this, will you?"

I smiled and stroked his cheek. "Okay. If that's what you want, then let's go."

Morten held the door for me and I got out of the car. We walked up towards the front entrance, hand in hand.

49

FEBRUARY 2014

We were only halfway through the main course when my phone rang. I pulled out my purse and grabbed the phone.

"It's Sophia," I said. "I'm sorry. I better take it. She knew I was going out and would never call if it wasn't important."

"Well, take it," Morten said.

"Thanks for understanding."

I picked it up. "Hello? Sophia?"

She sounded hysterical on the other end. "Emma I need you to come over here. I know you're out on a date and everything but..."

"Calm down, Sophia. Just tell me what happened." My eyes met with Morten's and I could tell he knew it was important.

"I...I was sitting in my living room...the kids...I think I had an encounter with your killer. The Caring Killer. The one I heard about on TV. I'm pretty sure he was here."

"What are you saying? How...? Are you sure?" I asked, startled.

"I'm pretty sure, yes. He was here in his ninja costume and everything. You need to come, Emma. I'm so scared. Don't tell Morten."

"What? Why not?"

"I'll explain when you get here. But please, just don't say anything. Please? Just come. I really need you."

"Okay. I'll be right there."

I hung up and looked at Morten.

"Guess that's the end of our romantic night, huh?" he said.

"I'm sorry. I'm so sorry, sweetie. Sophia needs me. She sounded really upset. I'm so sorry for ruining this beautiful night that you've arranged."

"It's nothing. I mean at least we got to the main course, right?" He sounded more upset than I think he realized. "So, what's the emergency?"

"Actually, she told me not to tell. I have no idea why, but it was important that I didn't tell anyone, apparently. I don't know. She was really upset, though."

"Well then, you'd better go to her."

"I'm sorry. Are you disappointed?"

Morten waved for the waiter to bring us the check. "Am I disappointed that I brought my girlfriend to a very expensive restaurant on a date that I saved up for for a long time? Am I disappointed that she wants us to leave half way through and that I don't even get to finish my meal? Well yes. I am a little disappointed. Who wouldn't be?"

"Oh, I feel so bad, Morten. Let me pay for the dinner. We'll do this again some other night?"

The check arrived and Morten put his credit card in the folded leather case. "Do you have any idea how hard it is to get reservations at a place like this?"

"Oh my. No I don't. I'm so so sorry. I've ruined everything haven't I?"

The waiter returned with Morten's card and he signed the receipt and thanked him. Morten got up and helped me get my coat on. "Let's just get you back to Sophia and find out what the emergency is."

"You're angry, aren't you?" I asked on our way back in the car. Morten hadn't spoken a word for a long time.

"I'm trying not to be," he said. "I mean, it's not your fault Sophia needs you in the middle of our dinner. But, it's just annoying. That's all."

"I know."

Morten drove up in front of Sophia's house. I leaned over and kissed him. The kiss felt flat.

"You wanna meet up at my place when I'm done here?" I asked. "You can wait for me in the bedroom, if you like."

"I don't think I'm in the mood, Emma. I'll call you in the morning."

"Okay," I said, disappointed.

I got out of the car and stood for a little while looking at him as he disappeared down the road. Then I turned and ran towards Sophia's front door.

50

SEPTEMBER 2007

Finally, the day arrived when Samuel was supposed to go to Hummelgaarden and meet with a counselor. Three days in a row, they had granted him. It wasn't much, but at least it was something, Alexandra thought happily as she dropped him off at the place. She wasn't supposed to go in with him, since this was supposed to be his place, his space where he could tell them what he wanted and be himself without thinking he needed to act in a certain way in order to please his mother. That was what they had told her.

She exhaled with relief as a tall man came out and greeted Samuel and took him inside. He waved at Alexandra to let her know everything was alright and that she could take off without worrying. She smiled and waved back, then watched as the door to the institution closed behind them.

Finally, he would get some help. Finally, she could get a break.

Things had been awful the last two months while they waited for an opening at Hummelgaarden. Poul didn't want to know of the boy and Samuel had started throwing his tantrums again, only now he had gotten bigger and stronger and that made it more difficult for us to handle him. He had thrown stuff around in the living room, trashed his own room completely, and kicked a hole in the bathroom door when Poul had locked him in there to calm down. The house was a wreck and so was Alexandra. She was crying herself to sleep again at night, not knowing what to do or how to deal with this and her doctor told her she had developed an ulcer. She needed to rest and not be stressed. It was affecting Olivia as well. She had a hard time breastfeeding and was crying more and more. Alexandra was up several times at night and could hardly keep herself together in the daytime. She was terrified of Samuel and what he might end up doing. She found herself trying to avoid spending time with him, which only made things worse and the tantrums come more often. She knew he felt neglected, she knew he wanted her to love him more than she did, but it was just so hard, so difficult with all they had gone through and the way he acted. There were just some things that time didn't seem to heal.

The people at Hummelgaarden had called Alexandra two weeks ago and she had talked to a guy who was going to be Samuel's counselor. He sounded nice, calm and very professional. He was also someone she felt she could share all of her concerns with and she was able to explain her situation to him without feeling like he condemned her in any way. Actually, he sounded like he completely understood her. For the first time since Samuel was four years old, there was someone who actually understood her! They were going to try different things with Samuel, he told her. Different kinds of therapy and see what he responded to.

"I've been with kids like Samuel before," he explained. "We don't have much time, but I'll make sure to use it the best way we can and get the most out of it."

Alexandra was so relieved when she hung up after the conversation with the counselor from Hummelgaarden and, for the first time in months, she actually had something to look forward to. She felt a slight hope grow in her that maybe there still was help for Samuel, that there was someone out there who could help him.

That was all she wished for. All she ever dreamed about. That he could have a normal life. That they could all have a normal life again.

Alexandra drove off with Olivia babbling in the backseat. She was still so small and fragile, but growing bigger by the day. She was so sweet and so gentle that Alexandra could hardly believe that she and Samuel had the same parents.

"Yes, Olivia. We'll pick him up tonight. Don't you worry."

Olivia loved her older brother. She was the only one in the family who adored him. He wasn't too fond of her, though. He couldn't stand it when she cried or fussed, and it would often make him scream even louder. But even though Samuel never talked much with her and never held her, it was like Olivia didn't care. She smiled when he looked at her and giggled even when he told her she *looked stupid*.

"Stupid baby," he always called her to her face.

But that only made her giggle even louder. Any attention from him was better than any Alexandra or Poul could give her. Alexandra didn't understand that, but she wondered if Olivia could somehow have a positive effect on Samuel. Maybe her unconditional love would help him understand that he was loved, even though his parents found it hard to show it?

Alexandra hoped. She was at the point where she hoped for anything and was willing to try everything. So when she was heading to pick up Samuel at the end of the day, she took Olivia along, even though Poul was home and asked if he shouldn't keep her.

When Samuel walked out of the building and the tall man gave him a hug, Alexandra gasped. Samuel never let anyone touch him anymore. This was a good sign.

She looked at Olivia. "Here comes your brother. Looks like he's made himself a new friend, doesn't it?"

The tall man waved at Alexandra with that friendly smile of his as Samuel approached the car. And what was that? He opened the door and he...he smiled!

"Hello, baby," he said and jumped inside the car.

No stupid? You always call her stupid baby.

To Alexandra's great surprise, he was still smiling as she watched him in the rearview mirror.

"Hi, Mom," he said.

Alexandra was about to burst into tears as she started the car. "How was your day, sweetie?"

"It was great, Mom. It was really great."

"I'm so glad to hear that, sweetie. Were they nice to you?" she asked, careful not to say anything that would set him off.

"Yes. They were. My counselor is awesome. Did you know he swims?"

"No. I didn't. I don't know much about him, to be honest."

"Yeah. He used to be like a pro swimmer. He won Bronze at the Olympics once. It was many years ago, but it's still pretty cool. I think swimming is pretty awesome, don't you?"

Alexandra tried to hold back her tears as she looked at him in the mirror once again. "I think it is very cool, yes."

"Me too. I think this was a very cool day too. Can't wait to go back there again tomorrow."

51

FEBRUARY 2014

"**W**HAT'S GOING ON?" Sophia opened the door and let me in. Inside, I found Jack, our other neighbor. "What's going on here?" I asked. "What's about the killer? And why can't I tell Morten? He needs to know about it if he's going to catch this guy."

"Sssophia met him tttonight. He was in hhhher house," Jack said.

"He was in here?"

She nodded. I noticed her hands were shaking. She sat down in an old chair. "I was sitting in my living room. I was watching TV and the kids had fallen asleep, when suddenly, someone just walked right through my front door."

"It wasn't locked. You never lock your door, Sophia!" I said. "I've told you a million times to lock it."

"I know. But things didn't used to be like this around here, you know? We used to be able to leave our homes unlocked and nothing would happen."

"But from now on, you're locking it, alright? Then what happened? Did he say anything?"

"He screamed. He was like a freaking ninja on speed. You have no idea how he yelled and screamed. He sounded exactly like my oldest when he's playing ninja turtle. It was so unreal, Emma. He was swinging his sword at me, telling me he was The Deliverer and that he was going to free me from my fears."

"That's exactly what he told that lady last night who was stabbed. He didn't hurt you?"

"Well, he was about to, but I shot him."

"You shot him?" I asked, my voice breaking.

"Yes, I shot him. Hit him in the shoulder. He screamed like a pig, then stormed out of the house. It woke up the kids and everything. Jack here heard it too and came running. He just put them all back to bed."

"But...but...good that nothing happened to you, but how...I mean, where did you get a gun?"

"See, that's why I didn't want you to blabber this to your boyfriend. After the last time my boyfriend sent me to the hospital, I bought a gun to be able to protect myself from future boyfriends. You know how I always fall for the bad guys. Well, I thought it was a good idea to get some protection, if you follow me."

"I do. Clearly. So you bought an illegal gun and now you're afraid you'll get in trouble if Morten finds out. I hear you loud and clear. Thank God you had it close at hand, though."

"I always keep it in this drawer, right next to my couch," she said and pointed at a dresser.

"What if one of the kids finds it?" I asked. You might want to find a more secure place."

"Hey. This thing just saved me from being sliced into pieces. I'll decide what is secure."

"Okay. We'll talk about this on a later occasion, but are you okay, Sophia? Do you need me to take you to the hospital?"

"He didn't hurt me. I'm more shocked than anything. That's why I called you...and I'm so glad Jack is here too. You guys are my closets friends. I needed you."

I leaned over and hugged Sophia. "I'm glad you did," I said. "And I'm glad you're alright. So you shot the bastard, huh? I bet he didn't see that coming."

Sophia chuckled. "No, he certainly didn't. You should have seen the look in his eyes when the bullet hit his shoulder. It was quite hilarious now that I think about it. I didn't think about anything other than protecting the kids when it happened, though. It was all that was on my mind. Kill him before he slaughters all your family. I'm glad a bullet through the shoulder was enough to scare him off. I'm a peace-loving person, you know? I would hate it if I had to kill someone. Even if it was to protect myself and my family."

I chuckled. "Yeah. I know. Do you want to sleep at my house? We could carry the kids over there."

"Nah. You have enough trouble as it is. I'm a big girl. I don't think the guy will dare to come back, do you?" Sophia asked and looked at the both of us.

Jack shook his head. "You ssscared him off pppretty good. He'll bbbe busy mending his wounds. He won't be bbback."

"I think you're safe," I said. "Do you want us to hang out here a little bit?"

"That would be nice. If you don't mind. I'm so sorry I ruined your romantic night," she said. "It's okay if you want to go back to Morten. I understand."

"Nah, that ship has sailed," I said and sat in a chair next to Sophia.

Jack sat on the couch.

"We'll stay here till you feel safe again. Right Jack?" I asked.

He smiled. "Rrright."

52

FEBRUARY 2014

Anders Samuelsen was bleeding. His shoulder was hurting like crazy and it hurt like hell to move his arm. When he ran out of that woman's house, he had been terrified. He heard her scream behind him and quickly looked for a place to hide across the street, so the crazy woman wouldn't follow after him and shoot him again.

He had been hiding there ever since...Not daring to walk into the street again. His heart was beating heavily in his painful chest as he hid in someone's yard across the street. He was sitting on the cold snow but soon figured he would only get sick if he stayed. So, he carefully rose to his feet and walked around the back of the two-story house. There was light coming out of the windows. Panting and moaning, Anders walked slowly up onto the back porch and looked inside.

An old man was sitting in an armchair. The TV was on, but he seemed to be asleep. Anders was freezing. His body was shivering. He was holding his sword with the arm that wasn't hurting. He looked down at it, resenting himself for having failed to fulfill his mission.

You'll have to kill him, Anders.

Careful to not make a sound, Anders grabbed the handle of one of the French doors and opened it. What a relief that it wasn't locked. Quiet as the ninjas he had read about online, he entered the living room and shut the door after him. Remembering step one in the article from Wiki-How called *How to Move like a Ninja*, he now made sure to maintain balance and control by *allowing his body weight to sink and be carried by deeply flexed knees.*

Anders had rehearsed this over and over in his house back then. Now, all his training finally came in handy.

Don't forget your breathing. Step two tells you that breathing is so important. You have to breathe along with your movement. Unconsciously holding your breath can unknowingly produce unneeded muscle tension and could result in a gasping release of breath if you are startled or accidentally unbalanced.

Anders focused on his breathing, while walking closer to the sleeping man in the chair, remembering step three: *Be as patient as possible.*

Don't rush it, Anders. Take as much time as you need. Impatience and the resultant hasty movement that it encourages are the greatest dangers to the person who must move silently without detection.

Anders calmed down by breathing regularly. When taking another step, he made sure to use all joints for movement, emphasizing fluidity through the engagement of the ankles, knees, and hips for stepping. In that way, he could avoid the lazy and dangerous habit of stiffening knees and swinging the entire leg from the hip.

But, first and foremost, he remembered to walk on his toes first, then roll onto his heel and, most important of all, he made sure to control his energy, *his chakra,* while he walked.

To his satisfaction, he didn't make a sound sneaking across the wooden planks. The old man in the chair had no idea what was coming towards him, he wasn't going to realize it until it was too late.

Anders tried hard not to giggle as he approached the old man in the green chair. The man was breathing heavily in his sleep. Anders imagined swinging the sword at him and cutting his throat. He wondered if it would be more effective to wake him up first? Have him look into Anders' eyes and realize what was about to happen? If he was to understand what was going on, it would definitely be best. He had to recognize his fear of death before embracing it, right?

Anders grunted slightly in pain as he lifted the sword with the good arm and stepped in front of the sleeping old man.

He was about to grab his shoulder and shake him, when suddenly there was a sound coming from the other side of the door. The sound of a key being turned. The voices of two people saying goodbye to each other outside. Anders felt how pearls of sweat sprang on his forehead and upper lip. He looked down at the old man. There was no way he could wake him up, kill him and then get away before the front door opened and someone would see him. If he stabbed the man in his sleep, he wouldn't get the maximum effect out of the whole thing. And that was, after all, the mission, wasn't it? To have them face their fear of death. To stare death into the eyes.

Anders stared at the door, then at the old man. He blinked his eyes several times. It was so hard to focus. It was like his brain was all blurry. He bit his lip, wondering where he even was and who the man in the chair was. He tried to listen to the voice in his head that had been guiding him the last several days now, the voice of whoever had sent him on this mission, but he couldn't hear it. He shook his head.

Don't fail me now. I need you. Don't leave me.

He looked up as the handle of the front door turned. And, just as the door was opening, he finally heard the voice again.

Run! Run for your life Anders.

Anders sprang up the stairs moaning and grunting in pain, found a bathroom and hid in the shower, pulling the curtain closed.

53

FEBRUARY 2014

Jack and I stayed with Sophia until she fell asleep on the couch. Then, we carried her into her bedroom and left the house, locking the door with my extra key that she gave me a long time ago.

"Ssso, you think she'll be alright?" Jack asked, as he walked me home.

I smiled and nodded. "He won't be back. She scared him to death by shooting him."

"Wouldn't he nnneed to go to the hhhospital?" Jack asked, as we reached my front door and stopped.

I shrugged. "I suppose."

I stared at Jack while wondering. If it really was The Caring Killer who had been shot, then we might actually have a possibility of catching him if he looked for help at the hospital in the mainland or at Dr. Williamsen's, our only doctor here. But then I'd have to tell Morten what happened, since he was the police and the only one who could ask the doctors to contact him if a patient with a gunshot wound showed up. I'd made a promise to Sophia, but if I kept quiet and kept it, I might lose a chance to finally catch the bastard.

It wasn't an easy decision.

"Anyway. I hhhave to get back and get my sister to bbbed," Jack said.

I looked at him and smiled. Always caring about his sister more than himself. When was it his turn to live? When she died? I loved that he took care of her the way he did, but couldn't stop wondering what might have been between us if it hadn't been for her. I loved his mysterious, artistic nature. He was so different from Morten.

"Well, thanks for helping us today," I said and found the key to my own door and put it in the lock.

"What are fffriends for?" he asked with a smile.

"See you later."

Jack waved and walked away. I watched him cross the road and walk towards his own house. Then I turned and opened the door.

"I'm home, Dad!" I yelled, took off my coat, and put it on a hanger. I placed it in the closet in the hallway, then pulled off my heavy boots. A small pile of snow landed on the wooden floors and started to melt slowly. I set them aside and walked into the living room where I found my father sleeping heavily in the old green chair that he loved so much. The TV was still on. I found the remote and turned it off. My dad woke when the noise from the TV stopped. He grunted and looked at me.

"What? Are you home already?"

"It's ten-thirty, Dad."

"Yeah, but on Valentine's Day...Aren't you kids supposed to stay out all night and go dancing and stuff?" he asked.

"Morten is not much of a dancer," I said.

My dad was scrutinizing me. "Something wrong with you two?"

"I don't know, Dad. It just kind of went wrong. Sophia called and needed my help, so I had to leave the dinner. Morten was really upset and left."

"Oh, that sounds bad. I'm sorry for that. What was so important with Sophia that it couldn't wait?"

"She had an emergency. I really promised not to say anything. Say, what is that on the floor?"

"What on the floor?" he asked perplexed.

"That over there. And there. It looks like..." I walked closer to the stains on my wooden floors. "It looks like small puddles of..." I kneeled to see better.

"Blood?"

My dad leaped out of the old chair and walked closer. "Blood?" he frowned. "That can't be right."

"The door to the yard is open," I said. "And there is blood on the floor? What happened here tonight?"

"I have no idea. Honestly, sweetie. I put Victor to bed around eight, then came down here and fell asleep watching *Shooting Star*. There was this kid who could sing exactly like Adele. It was really awesome, but then it got boring and I dozed off."

I looked at the bloodstains and realized they continued through the house towards the stairs. I even saw blood smeared on the railing of the stairs. I was about to walk up, when I heard a voice coming from outside the door. In came Maya and my mother, looking cheerful and happy.

"Wow, it's a party in here?" my mother asked. She was a little tipsy.

Maya laughed. "We met downtown and shared a cab," she said. "What's going on here?"

"There's blood on the floor," my dad said.

My mom blew raspberries, then laughed. "Blood. That sounds like something from one of your books, Emma. It's probably just mud or ketchup. Maybe Victor spilled ketchup on the floor? You have to relax, sweetheart. You're way too tense. Loosen up a little will you?"

"As soon as I make sure Victor is alright, I will," I said and stormed up the stairs.

54

FEBRUARY 2014

I had a bad feeling about this whole situation as I approached Victor's room. Something had happened to Victor. I just knew it. I sensed it.

I grabbed the handle and opened the door to his room. My heart stopped. Everything inside of me froze.

He wasn't there. Victor wasn't in his bed.

"Victor?"

I rushed in and checked everywhere in the room, calling out his name.

"Victor?"

His bed was messed up. It wasn't right. He always made his bed very neatly when he wasn't in it. So, he had been sleeping in it. But the covers were on the floor. The sheet was messed up. Something was really wrong here. Frantically, I searched his room, under the bed, his closet, everything, but found no trace of him. My heart was racing heavily as I tried to think of where he could be.

"The bathroom."

I ran into the hall and opened the door. "Victor?" I asked, my voice shaking heavily with angst.

"Victor? Are you in here?"

But there was no answer. He wasn't on the toilet. I looked at the shower curtain. It was pulled aside. Could he be hiding behind it? Maybe he had a bad dream? Maybe something had scared him?

"Victor?"

I was about to grab the curtain when a voice coming from the door stopped me. It was Maya.

"Mom?"

I looked at her. She could see the fear written on my face. It scared her. "What's going on, Mom?"

"I...I can't find Victor."

"What?"

"He's...he's not in his room and he's not in here either. Do you have any idea where he can be?" I asked. "Does he maybe have a secret hide-out I don't know about?"

"Only the yard. He loves to play there, but you know all about that. You think he might have gone into the yard at night?"

"I don't know. Right now, I'm willing to believe anything. I'm so scared, Maya. I'm so afraid that something might have happened to him. I mean there was blood on the floor in the living room for Christ sake. Was that his blood? What the heck is going on here?"

Maya grabbed my hand and pulled me closer, then she hugged me. "Mom you have to relax. It won't help anyone if you panic."

"You're right, sweetie. I'm so sorry. I just feel so..."

"Helpless?"

I nodded. That was exactly how I felt. It was the most awful feeling in the world. As a mother, I was used to always knowing what to do. But this time, I didn't. I was so struck by fear over what might have happened to him that I could hardly move.

"He's so fragile, Maya. The world will tear him apart if he's left alone out there. I have to find him."

"Let's go downstairs and talk to the others. Then, we'll send out a search team," Maya said with great authority. It would have made me very proud if I hadn't been so paralyzed by fear.

She grabbed me around the shoulder and, together, we left the bathroom and went down the stairs. My mom and dad were arguing downstairs when we got down.

"Can't you ever just take anything seriously, Ulla," my dad said. I could hear a deep anger in his voice. It came from years of frustration that finally was allowed to come to the surface.

"Oh come on," my mother said. "Emma is always so tense. She gets it from you, you know. You both need to learn how to relax. She's always fussing about the boy. She's always so tense about him. No wonder he's weird and can't do anything on his own. Boys don't need you to fuss about them. They need to be independent and stand on their own two feet. He's fine, I tell you."

As my mom spoke the last words, she turned and looked into my eyes. Then she blushed.

"Emma...I..."

"He's not fine, Mom. Victor is not fine at all. He's gone."

55

SEPTEMBER 2007

Alexandra couldn't believe how fast the three days went by. It had been the best three days of her life, she thought, when she drove up in front of Hummelgaarden on the last day to pick up Samuel.

She looked at Olivia in the back seat. She was staring at the car door with great anticipation. Her legs and arms were kicking wildly with expectation.

"He'll be here in a minute, sweetie. I know you're looking forward to seeing him. So am I."

It was the truth. For the first time in many years, Alexandra had actually enjoyed her son's company. He had been so sweet and gentle to be around on all three days of his counseling and Alexandra was so sad it was all over now. She was worried that everything was going to go back to what it was before. No...worried was too mild a word. She was petrified.

She studied Olivia's smiling eyes while they both waited for Samuel to step inside the car. In the three days, the two of them had managed to build up something, a relationship of some sort that Alexandra had never even dared to hope for between the two of them. Samuel had played with his baby sister, laughed, and even kissed her. It had been quite extraordinary.

But now what? Now that it was all over, what was going to happen next? She wanted to ask the counselor, but knew she had to go through the social worker first. Alexandra wanted to schedule an appointment for her to go see him and talk to him and know what it was he had done to change Samuel so drastically. She wanted tricks if he had any. Or just plain good advice. He was the first person ever to have reached Samuel and managed to change his ways.

But Alexandra wasn't even sure they would ever let her have an appointment with the counselor. It turned out to be a lot harder than she expected when she had called earlier in the day to talk to Marianne Moeller about it. She wanted to ask her if it was okay if she walked inside Hummelgaarden today to pick up Samuel and maybe chat a little with the counselor that Samuel had been with. She never thought it would cause a problem, but apparently it did. Marianne Moeller had told her in many harsh words that Hummelgaarden was a very busy place and they couldn't have all kinds of parents running around up there wanting *to chat with the counselors.* She would only be disturbing and upsetting all the patients. They weren't comfortable with strangers. So, no. She wasn't allowed to go inside.

Alexandra had her doubts as to whether they would make her an appointment, but how else would she get to talk to the man? He apparently knew something Alexandra could use.

"We have very strict regulations that we have to follow," Marianne Moeller had said.

Alexandra didn't care much for all their regulations and rules. All she wanted was a little help. Was that too much to ask? But the social worker had suddenly started talking about her not being cooperative enough and telling her she didn't care for her attitude and that was when Alexandra knew she had to hang up before she said anything she would later regret.

Now, she spotted Samuel as he came out of the front door. The tall male counselor was with him. Now they were shaking hands. The counselor pulled him closer and gave him a warm hug. Alexandra almost cried when she saw it. Samuel was smiling and hugging the man back.

What was it that man could do?

Alexandra couldn't just sit here and watch. Here was this man, so close to her car and all she wanted was to talk to him. He was, after all, outside the building, so she wasn't overstepping any rules and regulations was she?

Alexandra didn't care. While Samuel and the counselor talked, she jumped out of the car, grabbed Olivia from the backseat and walked up towards them with a smile, acting like it was the most natural thing in the world. She walked straight up to them and reached out her hand towards the counselor.

"Hi. I'm Alexandra, Samuel's mom. We spoke on the phone a couple of days ago. You must be Ole Knudsen. I just want to thank you for all you've done for my son. Whatever it is you've been doing, it has changed his life and ours completely in only three days."

Ole nodded. "Well it has been my pleasure. Samuel is a good boy. He just needs to believe in himself more, believe that he can control that anger and that he is loved. He has a great family. He has told me so many wonderful things about you."

Alexandra almost burst into tears. She could hardly believe it. "Really? He said nice things about us?"

"Yes. Samuel is a very sensitive boy. He has a lot of love for the people around him. He just needs to reach into that place deep inside of here," he said and pointed at Samuel's heart. "With the right tools, he will one day be able to control that temper."

"And what tools are they?" Alexandra asked hopefully.

"Well that'll probably take a lot of counseling to help him figure out exactly what will help him. I will recommend in his report that he'll need to start a weekly session here."

Alexandra's face lit up. "That would be so great. He would love that, wouldn't you, Samuel?"

"The only problem is the waiting list," Ole said. "It might be six months to a year before we can start."

Alexandra's heart dropped. "Six months to a year? That's a really long time. He might forget everything you've taught him by then. What if he gets himself into trouble while we wait?"

"Well, I certainly hope he won't. But I have thought of a solution, one that might help ease the wait."

"What is that?"

"I don't know if Samuel told you, but I used to be a professional swimmer."

"Yes, he told me that."

"Great. Samuel has told me he would like to start swimming on a regular basis. I have talked to him about the importance of exercise and he thinks swimming is the perfect choice for him. I think so too. So, I was wondering if you'd mind me teaching him, let's say once a week? I could take him to the local indoor pool and train him. Then maybe we could talk for a little while afterwards. I can't call it counseling, since I'm not allowed to counsel outside of work, but I'm guessing he might enjoy talking a little to an old friend or a swim teacher. What do you say? Would that be something you would allow him to do?"

Alexandra stared at the tall man. She couldn't believe what he was saying. Could this be true? Was he really being understanding and offering her and Samuel help?

"As I said, I really believe he is a good boy," Ole said. "I really think I will be able to help him. And you."

"Mom?" Samuel said. "Can we do it?"

For the first time in years, Alexandra smiled from ear to ear. Tears were rushing down her cheeks as she spoke.

"Well, of course, sweetie. Of course you can do it."

56

FEBRUARY 2014

I called Morten as soon as we'd searched the house and the yard and still couldn't find Victor. I didn't care that our evening ended badly or that he might still be mad at me.

"I need your help," I said. "Victor is missing. I don't know what to do."

"Take it easy, Emma. Stay where you are. I'll be right there."

Three minutes later, he stormed through my front door. "Emma. Are you alright? How are you?"

"I'm scared," I said. "I found blood on the living room floor. I'm afraid something bad happened to him. Something really bad."

"Let's not jump to conclusions here," Morten said and hugged me. "Now let's go through everything. Could he have wandered off on his own?"

I shook my head in despair. "I don't know. Who knows what goes on in his head? But no, he has never done anything like that before."

"Did he seem upset tonight in any way?" Morten asked my dad.

My dad shrugged. "I...no, not really. He was very quiet and didn't say much, but that's not that unusual. I don't know."

"You told me he's been having trouble in school lately. Maybe that could have affected him in some way?" Morten asked.

"Maybe," I said, frantically searching my brains for answers. "But what about the blood? How do you explain the blood?"

"I think I better make some calls," Morten said and grabbed his phone. "We'll have to form a search team. You better call anyone you know as well."

Half an hour later, the street was packed with people, some in uniform others just friends and neighbors who wanted to help. Morten directed them and they divided the city and the forest and beach-area up between them. In groups, they started walking hand in hand, calling Victor's name.

I was moved by the turnout. Most of these people hardly even knew us. Maya had joined one of the groups. Jack was coordinating the team going towards town, while Sophia couldn't leave her children, but hugged me tightly and asked if there was anything else she could do for me.

"It's okay, Sophia. I have plenty of people to help me out. But thanks."

"Okay. But let me know, alright?"

"You stay at the house, Emma," Morten said and kissed me on the forehead. "In case he finds his way back home on his own."

I nodded and bit my lip. Morten looked into my eyes. "We will find him. Don't you worry, okay? Everything will be fine."

I cleared my throat. "Okay."

I watched as Morten and a group of policemen with dogs walked towards the beach. My dad put a hand on my shoulder. "Come on inside, sweetie. Your mom will make some coffee."

I put my head on my dad's shoulder and let him hold me tight while we walked back to the kitchen where my mother had started filling the pot with water. "I'll make the real stuff this time," she said with a smile.

"Is there anything else we can get you?" my dad asked.

I shook my head. "No. But thanks. Coffee will be great."

It was strange sitting in the kitchen with both my mom and dad quietly sipping coffee. I couldn't remember when they had last been in the same room. I couldn't remember when I had last been together with the both of them. And they weren't even arguing anymore. If it hadn't been under these circumstances, I think I would have enjoyed it. Apparently, they couldn't agree on much, but when it came to taking care of their daughter, they managed to hold aside their differences. It felt good to have them with me. It was comforting.

Three hours later and still no news. Morten had called a couple of times to make sure I was alright and to hear if anyone else had called back with news, but there was none. Another hour went by and slowly most of the search teams came back. Tired and long faces appeared in our driveway and we served them coffee and sandwiches as a thank you. They were sad and some even tried to apologize for not having found my son.

"Well, you did all you could," I told them with a heavy voice before they went home to get some sleep.

Morten and his group came back half an hour later and, by then, all the other search teams had come back and left again with no results. I was sitting in the hallway with my back against the wall hiding my face in my hands when he entered.

"Emma?"

I looked at him with the last ray of hope in my eyes, but as I looked into his eyes, I knew he hadn't found Victor either.

"I'm sorry," he said. "We searched all the beaches and the dunes and the plantation behind it, but still nothing. We'll continue in the morning, but I have to let my team get some rest."

"Of course," I said with a thick voice.

"You should get some sleep too. I'll stay here with you, if you like."

I looked up at him. "I would very much like that, thank you."

57

FEBRUARY 2014

Naturally, we didn't sleep at all. Morten and I lay close together in the bed, holding each other in the darkness, while I kept wondering where Victor could be. There was no way he had left the house on his own. I was almost certain of that. At six in the morning, I turned the light on and looked at Morten.

"I think I know who took him," I said.

Morten rubbed his eyes. "Who?"

"The Caring Killer, of course. Why didn't I think of that before? I thought he was too hurt to have anything to do with this, since Sophia shot him, but what if he wasn't badly hurt? What if he managed to get himself into the house and grab Victor? That would explain the blood."

Morten shook his head. "What? Could you go back a little? The Caring Killer was here? And you didn't tell me? And Sophia did what? Was that her emergency?"

"Yes. I promised to not tell you. He tried to attack her tonight in his ninja costume and she shot him. He ran off and that's when she called me. Oh my God. He must have run across the street to my house. He must have come into my yard and into the house through the porch and snuck upstairs to take Victor!"

"So Sophia has an illegal gun at her house...that was why you couldn't tell me, huh? It was a really stupid choice to keep it a secret. I mean, the killer was here on your street. I could have caught him, for crying out loud." Morten calmed himself down by taking a deep breath. "Where did she hit him?"

"In the shoulder."

"Well, I guess he could have continued even if he was shot in the shoulder. Being shot in the shoulder isn't fatal. So you think he took Victor to get back at her or something? What was he even doing in Sophia's house?"

"I have no idea. I have completely lost track of why he does anything. In the beginning, it was all calculated and he seemed so intelligent, now it seems more coincidental. Maybe you're right, after all. Maybe he is just another maniac. Maybe he went in the wrong house when he attacked Sophia? I mean, he's been using me all this time, so maybe it was his plan to attack me instead?"

"It doesn't sound like him to make a mistake like that," Morten said.

"No, it doesn't. I don't understand it either, but I'm sure of one thing. The Caring Killer has taken Victor."

I jumped out of bed and put my pants back on, then ran a brush through my hair. I felt how the anger was growing inside of me rapidly. I really hated this guy and I was going to find him and make him pay for all he had done.

"If he hurts Victor in any way...I'll, well, I'll...I'll shoot him myself," I snorted in anger.

I felt Morten's hand on my shoulder. He put his arms around me and held me close to him for a long time. I closed my eyes and tried to calm myself down.

"I'm so sorry that you have to go through all this," he said. "It makes me so angry. We'll find him and Victor. I make that promise to you right now. I'll have all my colleagues working on it today. We will find them both. If I have to follow him to the end of the world in order to stop him, I will. I'm not letting him get away with this."

I turned around and kissed Morten. Tears were rolling down my cheeks. "Why is he doing this to me? Why me?"

"I don't know, Emma. I don't know why he chose you, of all people. He's a ruthless killer. A psychopath. You never know what they'll do next. But I will make sure it's the last thing he does in freedom. I give you my word.

Morten kissed me gently before we walked downstairs and he put on his jacket. "I'll go to the station right away," he said.

"Don't you want a cup of coffee first?" I asked.

He shook his head. "No. I can't think about coffee right now. I just want to catch the bastard. I saw Morten off, then walked into the living room where I found my mom and dad both lying on the couch, sound asleep, my dad's arm around my mom's shoulder. It made me smile for the first time in many hours.

58

FEBRUARY 2014

He had heard everything. Anders Samuelsen had followed the situation from his hideout in the bathroom of the old house. At first, he had watched Emma Frost come inside and call for Victor, who he guessed was her son. As she had grabbed the curtain and was about to pull it aside, Anders had prepared himself to kill her. He had lifted the sword and was ready to strike as soon as she pulled the curtain aside, but for some reason, she had stopped. Then, he had heard another voice and seen the girl, the daughter. He listened to Emma talk to her daughter about him, about how she couldn't find the son.

When they searched the house, he hid in a cupboard underneath the sink in the bathroom listening to the voices calling the boy's name and the desperation in Emma's voice. He sensed how tense and fear-filled Emma was. He was getting sensitive to these things.

He was surprised that it was her house he had entered, but as time went by, he was more and more certain that it was no coincidence. There was a plan to it all.

Anders stayed in the small cupboard for hours and hours. It

was way too small for him, but he had squeezed himself into a small ball, like a true ninja would, and no one would ever suspect that he was in the cupboard, since they would never suspect that any human being would be able to fit in there.

Now that the house had gone quiet and had been for a long time, Anders carefully opened the cupboard door and peeked out. It was light outside now, so night had become day. Anders moaned in pain as he crawled out of the small cupboard. His shoulder still hurt like crazy, but he was getting better at pushing through the pain. The bleeding seemed to have stopped.

He rolled out onto the bathroom floor like small ball and slowly unfolded his sore body. Once he was back on his feet, he stuck his hand behind the bathtub where he had hidden his sword and pulled it out. He attached it to his back, looked at himself in the mirror to make sure his face was still covered, then smiled underneath the black cloth.

Today was a good day for people to die.

Anders sneaked out of the bathroom and down the stairs, then he stopped because he heard voices coming from the hallway. He sneaked closer and watched as Emma Frost said goodbye to someone, then closed the front door. He studied her in secret as she walked into the living room and saw how she smiled when she saw the two elderly people sleeping on the couch. Yet, despite the smile, he could sense how fragile she was at this moment, how tense and fearful she was. She wasn't the same Emma he had seen that day in the cemetery.

What are you so afraid of, Emma-dearest? What makes your heart ache?

Emma found a blanket on a chair and put it over the two people that were sleeping. Then she walked back towards the kitchen with heavy steps. As she turned the corner, Anders hid behind a door. He watched her through the kitchen door that wasn't closed properly. She was sitting on a chair, her elbows resting on the table, hiding her face in her hands. Oh, how it hurt him to see her like this. That was when the voice returned.

You have to do something, Anders. You're the only one who can. You have to save her.

While watching Emma cry into her hands, Anders realized little by little what the plan was...what the purpose for him coming back from the dead really was. It was all about her wasn't it? It had to be.

She needs you Anders. She needs your help.

Of course she did. It went without saying. It was so simple, really. She had helped him get out of the ground, she had helped him get back to life, now he was to return the favor.

59

FEBRUARY 2014

B jarne Norregaard was whistling on his way to work. It was a cold morning, one of those he enjoyed immensely. Many people didn't like the long dark Danish winters, but Bjarne wasn't one of them. He loved the clear blue sky and the white snow and the crisp icy air nipping at his nose and cheeks.

Nothing could beat that, Bjarne thought happily to himself.

He parked his bike and walked through the snow towards the back entrance of Citybanken. As the manager, he was supposed to get in before they opened the doors to the public. He was the one who held the key and who opened all the doors, so he had to be the first one there.

Bjarne typed the security code in and turned the alarm off, then found the key and put it in the lock and turned it. He walked inside and closed the door behind him. Still whistling, he walked towards his office in the back and put his briefcase on the desk. Oh how he loved these quiet mornings in the back before the day really started. This day he was particular happy since Bjarne had just learned that he was going to be a grandfather. His daughter Laura was expecting a baby in August. Bjarne and his wife had almost given up hope of ever becoming grandparents, since Laura and her husband had tried for years with no results. Now, after all kinds of fertility treatments, they had finally conceived.

"If it's a boy, we'll name him Bjarne after you, Dad," Laura had said.

That had made Bjarne cry and now, thinking about it, he cried a little again. It was such an honor.

As usual, Bjarne turned on his computer, then looked at the clock on the wall. Ten minutes till his employees arrived. Ten more minutes of peace. Bjarne took in a deep breath and enjoyed the silence. Soon, all five of his employees would be sitting at their desks outside his office, working, typing, and talking on the phone with clients. The entire bank would buzz with activity.

He was going to tell them before they opened the doors. He was going to gather all of them and tell them the great news. Then, he would run to the bakery in the afternoon and buy an *Othellolagkage*. The best cake you could get, in Bjarne's opinion. And the most expensive. But it was worth it. This was a day to celebrate.

Bjarne walked into the empty front room of the bank where all his employees would be sitting in just a short while. He rehearsed what he was going to say over and over again. Then he stopped.

What was that? Was there something on the floor? Or was it... was it some*one*? Was there a person lying on the floor of the bank?

Bjarne's heart started racing in his chest. In the twenty-four years he had been the manager of this bank, nothing like this had ever happened. He had no idea how to react.

"Hello?" Bjarne stuttered, nervously.

He walked slowly closer, but was uncertain if he should simply stop and walk back and call for the police. It looked like the body of a small boy.

"Hello?" he asked again and walked closer, driven by his curiosity. "What are you doing in here?"

A thousand thoughts ran through his mind as he walked closer.

Was the boy dead? He was lying awfully still, wasn't he? Was he lifeless? Was he sleeping?

"Hello?" Bjarne asked again, as he came all the way up to the boy's body. "Are you alright?"

The boy was lying on his back and now he opened his eyes. Bjarne breathed a sigh of relief. He had followed the story of The Caring Killer closely in the media and thought for a second it was another of his victims. The boy looked at Bjarne with confusion.

"What are you doing in here?" Bjarne asked.

The boy didn't answer. Bjarne wondered if he even understood Danish. "You're not supposed to be in here," he continued anyway.

The boy moved and tried to sit up, but couldn't get upright. That was when Bjarne realized he had something around his chest, underneath his PJs. It looked like a vest of some sort.

Bjarne's heart stopped. "What's that you have there, boy? What is that attached to you?" he asked with a shivering voice.

"Oh my God," he said. "Is that...is that...a bomb?"

The boy still didn't say anything. He wasn't even looking at Bjarne.

"Let me see," Bjarne said, grabbing the boy's shirt and pulling it up.

That was when the boy started screaming.

60

FEBRUARY 2014

*H*ow can I just sit here and do nothing?
The question came into my mind again and again as I sat in the kitchen alone, wondering if my life was ever going to be the same again.

I need to do something. I need to drive around town and call his name, ask people if they've seen him. I need to at least do something.

But Morten had told me the police were going to do all that. They were going to search all over town. He wanted me to stay at the house in case Victor came back or in case The Caring Killer tried to contact me.

I felt helpless. Useless. I was scared senseless and was constantly going back and forth on what to do. I was furious and wanted to act at one moment, then terrified and almost paralyzed the next. It was no use. No matter what I did, if I stayed or left to search for Victor, I would always blame myself afterwards for doing the wrong thing if I lost him. I would never forgive myself.

My mom came into the kitchen after half an hour or so and sat next to me. She put her arm around my shoulder. We sat like this for a while without saying a word. It felt nice. I was so glad she was there.

"It's just so frustrating," I said. "I can't stand the waiting."

Suddenly, my phone rang. I grabbed it.

"Hello?"

A voice that was obviously distorted sounded machinelike on the other end. "It's horrifying when you don't know what has happened to your child, isn't it?"

My heart stopped. "Who are you? Where is my son?"

"Did you know that every year, three mentally ill people get killed because they're considered dangerous? Last year, a man was shot dead on a train because he was yelling and screaming inside a train car. And, when the police arrived, they didn't know what to do or how to get him out of the train. They claim they thought he was armed, but he wasn't carrying any weapons. They shot and killed him on the spot because they claimed he was being threatening. Later, it turned out he was schizophrenic. What if he was just scared? What if his mind tricked him so badly that he was terrified?"

"I don't know where you're going with all this. And, frankly, I don't care. I'm sick of these games. I'm sick of you. So you want to focus on the mentally ill and their problems, I get it. Find another way to do it. Leave me and my family alone. I want my son back and I want him back now. Where is he?"

The voice laughed on the other end of the line. It gave me the chills.

"I swear, if you have hurt him in any way..."

"Then what, Emma?" The voice hissed. "Then you'll kill me, is that it? Well, I'm already dead. Don't you realize that?"

"Where is my son?"

"Turn on the TV."

"What?"

"You heard me."

I fumbled around and found the remote for my small kitchen

TV, then turned it on. A reporter was talking. On the screen it said *Breaking News. Robbery at Citybanken going on right now. Witnesses say a boy with a bomb is inside.*

"What have you done?" I asked.

"Tag, you're it," he said, still laughing, then hung up.

I stared at the TV screen.

"What's going on?" my mother asked. "Who was that on the phone?"

"I don't have time, Mom. I need to go into town immediately. Call Morten and tell him to meet me at Citybanken. Tell him I found Victor. He's inside the bank."

61

The last four months had been going so well. Alexandra could hardly believe it. Samuel was swimming every week with the counselor from Hummelgaarden and he was like a changed child. Every Wednesday, he came home from the pool happy. It was such a joy. It had changed Alexandra's life drastically.

She was still homeschooling him and they still had their problems, but it was nothing compared to how it used to be. The tantrums were fewer and, when they occurred, it seemed Samuel was slowly learning how to control them and his anger. Samuel was making eye contact with his parents when he spoke to them. His tics disappeared and, slowly, they were getting him off his medications.

Ole was working with him on something he called Energywork, where he talked to Samuel about the negative thoughts and patterns that caused his bad behavior and the anger. Slowly, Samuel regained control of himself and Alexandra recognized that sweet boy she had loved so much. Samuel learned energy exercises enabling him to control his thoughts and body. He began using what Ole called "a loving energy" as a tool to shift his consciousness from dark thoughts into the light. Alexandra and Poul both thought it sounded strange, but as soon as they saw the results in Samuel, they didn't care anymore. It didn't matter how Ole did it or why it worked, as long as it did. As long as they had their son back.

Four months later they were called in for a meeting with the social worker at City Hall. Alexandra was really looking forward to it.

"I hope they've found a spot for Samuel at Hummelgaarden," she said in the car on their way there.

They had left the kids at Alexandra's mom's house in order to be able to go there and talk to the social worker alone.

"I think that's why they want to see us, don't you?" she asked hopefully. "Oh it's going to be so good. Finally, we have some good luck, huh?"

"Let's hope so," Poul said and parked the car.

They walked up to City Hall and were shown into Marianne Moeller's office where they sat down. Two women were present there. One was Marianne Moeller, the other presented herself as Tine Solvang.

"Tine is my supervisor," Marianne said. "She wanted to be present for this, since this concerns all of us."

Alexandra felt a knot in her stomach as she looked into their serious faces. What was going on here? This didn't look like happy news.

Marianne Moeller cleared her throat. "So, we have been informed that your son has been seeing Ole Knudsen on a regular basis. Is that correct?"

Alexandra looked at Poul, then at the two women. "Yes. That's correct. It has been such a blessing for us..."

"That might be, but it's against the rules," Tine Solvang interrupted.

"I beg your pardon?"

"The counselors are not allowed to see patients privately," Marianne Moeller said. "This is a very serious breach of our regulations and will not be tolerated. It cannot continue."

"Excuse me?" Alexandra said.

"Your son can no longer see Ole Knudsen."

"But...but, all they do is to swim together. How can you have anything against that?"

"Ole Knudsen is not allowed to socialize with patients outside of his workplace. Those are the rules."

"But...," Alexandra was about to cry and looked to Poul for help.

"You can't be serious," Poul said. "These swimming lessons have meant the world to us, to our family. Ole has been so great with Samuel. He has changed him completely. Samuel loves spending time with him. All they do is swim, for crying out loud."

"That might be, but he is not allowed to do that. We have given him a reprimand and, if he is seen with the boy again, then he knows he will lose his job."

Marianne Moeller collected her paperwork in a pile. "That's the way it's going to be."

"But...but...what are we supposed to do?" Alexandra asked.

Marianne Moeller shrugged. "Well, that's really not our problem, is it?"

62

FEBRUARY 2014

A huge crowd had gathered outside of Citybanken. I parked my car and ran towards the building. A couple of officers had surrounded the bank and were pointing their weapons at the entrances. I didn't recognize any of the officers and realized it had to be some of those that had been send over from the mainland to assist Morten and his colleagues on the case of The Caring Killer.

I tried to get closer, but was stopped by one of them.

"Don't come any closer. There is a bomb inside of that building," he said.

"Is there a boy in there too?" I asked with a shivering voice.

"Yes, there is."

"I think it might be my son."

The officer suddenly looked at me. He let me through the police tape and led me to another officer, who he told me was the leader of the team.

"So, it's your son who's in there?" the leader asked.

"Yes. I believe it is. He went missing last night...I...is he alright?"

"Well, let's see...He is in the middle of robbing a bank and has taken the manager hostage in there. You're asking if he is alright? I don't think I care much about that right now."

"I beg your pardon?" I asked and looked at the officer, terrified. "Victor would never do anything like that."

"That's what all parents say. Nevertheless, that's what's happening here. Your son is in the bank with a bomb around his chest, holding the manager hostage."

"Have you tried to talk to him?" I asked.

"We have. But it's impossible. He keeps screaming. It was an employee that discovered them this morning when he got to work. He heard the boy screaming and looked through the window and saw the manager on the floor, lying with his arms over his head, yelling for the boy to spare his life."

"But, Victor would never threaten anyone," I argued. This was all so strange. How could Victor threaten anyone? He lived in a world of his own and didn't care anything about money.

"Can I talk to him?"

"Yes. Please do. But, be careful. I'll get you the megaphone."

"No. I want to go in there and talk to him. Face to face."

"That's not possible. He is way too dangerous," the officer said.

"My son is not dangerous. It's all just a big misunderstanding."

"I believe he has a history of mental illness, is that true?" the officer asked.

"Yes, that is true. But that doesn't mean he is dangerous."

"But it does mean he can be quite unpredictable, am I right? Has he acted threateningly before? Someone told me he recently showed pictures of decapitated heads in school, is that right?"

Oh my God. I can't believe this guy.

"Listen. Victor is eight years old. Yes, he has his issues, but he is not dangerous. Now would you please let me walk in there and talk to my son? You know what? I don't care if you let me do it or not. I'm going in there whether you want me to or not. You'll have to shoot me to stop me."

I turned on my heel and started walking.

"Wait," the officer yelled after me.

I didn't stop. Nothing and no one was going to stop me from getting to my son and saving him from this situation. The officer ran after me and caught up with me.

"I'm sending two of my men in with you," he said.

I snorted as my answer and continued my walk towards the back entrance of the bank. The two officers were right behind me as I grabbed the door and pulled it open.

63

FEBRUARY 2014

I could hear Victor screaming when I opened the door. I spotted him in the middle of the room, where he was standing with his hands covering his ears, screaming at the top of his lungs. On the floor, I saw the manager on his knees, pleading for his life.

"Please. I'm about to become a grandfather. Please, just let me go."

I looked at Victor and saw that he was having one of his many tantrums. "Victor," I said. "Victor, calm down, sweetie."

Victor stopped screaming. He didn't look at me, but kept staring at the floor. He seemed to have drawn back into his own world and that was when it was so difficult to reach him. It often happened when he was scared or emotional, like when his dad left us. I breathed deeply, being careful not to scare him.

I reached down and tapped the manager on the shoulder. "You can leave now," I said. "I've got him. He never meant to harm you."

The manager looked at me, then at Victor before he rushed out the door, whimpering. I heard people applaud when he got outside.

This is not happening. This is not happening to us.

The two officers were still pointing their guns at Victor and I had to choose my words and moves very carefully. Besides, I had no idea where the detonator to the bomb was or if it might go off at any moment. Was there a timer on it, like in the movies? Or was the killer waiting to get me close enough before he detonated it and killed all of us? I tried hard not to think about it.

"Victor?" I said. "Victor, buddy. It's me."

He didn't move and still didn't look at me.

"Look at me, Victor. Please, just look at me."

Finally, he lifted his head and looked into my eyes. "There you go, buddy. Now I'm going to get closer to you and take a look at that vest you're wearing, alright? We need to get it off of you before something bad happens, alright?"

Victor started humming. That was a bad sign. He was scared. The officer to my right reacted abruptly.

"Don't," I said. "No sudden moves. He's scared to death. That's why he hums."

I walked closer with my hand stretched out towards Victor. "I'm coming closer now. And I need to touch you, Victor. I know you don't like that, but I have to. I need to get the vest off of your body. Can I do that? Am I allowed to touch you Victor?"

He didn't answer, but I moved closer anyway. I figured there wasn't much time to lose. I had to move fast. I reached out and grabbed his shirt and pulled it up to better see.

Next thing, Victor screamed again. Hysterically, he screamed at the top of his lungs. Out of the corner of my eye, I saw the officer to my left hurry forward, pointing his gun at Victor and yelling in panic.

"He's gonna detonate the bomb!"

"Doooon't!" I screamed.

It happened in a split second and there was no way I could have acted differently. The police officer moved his finger on the trigger and was about to shoot at Victor when I jumped him and the shot went off into the roof with a loud sound.

It was pure chaos after that. Victor was screaming even louder now, the officer was yelling at me. I got up and ran to Victor, then without caring how loud he screamed or how much he cried, I pulled off his shirt and tore off the vest. I threw it on the floor, lifted Victor into my arms and carried him outside.

The crowd went silent when I came out carrying my son in my arms. I spotted Morten next to the officer in charge. I walked towards him.

"Are you alright?" he asked.

"The bomb is still inside," I said. "Now, if you'll excuse me. I'm taking my son home."

64

JANUARY 2008

They had to tell him. But how? Alexandra and Poul had discussed it all the way back from City Hall.

"It's going to break his heart," Alexandra had said.

They decided to wait till after dinner. They picked Samuel and Olivia up at Alexandra's mom's place and drove home, then Alexandra prepared all of Samuel's favorite dishes and put Olivia to bed.

With a heavy heart, she walked downstairs where Poul and Samuel were watching TV. She stopped at the end of the stairs and watched them sitting on the couch together. They too had become closer the last several months. Alexandra had never thought they would be this close again; she had almost given up on them, but ever since Ole had started counseling Samuel, that too had changed.

Was he strong enough to be on his own now? Would he be able to use the techniques that Ole had taught him on his own when things were bad?

"Damn those stupid rules and regulations," Alexandra grumbled.

She took in a deep breath, then walked into the living room. Poul turned off the TV. Samuel looked at Alexandra.

"We need to talk," she said. "Your dad and I have something important to tell you."

Samuel looked confused. "What? I didn't do anything wrong, did I?"

Alexandra smiled and shook her head. "No sweetie. This is not your fault. You're fine. You have been very good lately."

"And we know that a lot of it has to do with Ole and the time you're spending with him," Poul continued.

Alexandra exhaled deeply. How she hated this moment. How she loathed having to do this to the boy.

"Then what is it?" Samuel asked. "What's going on?"

"It hurts me to have to tell you this, Sammy, but I'm afraid you can't see Ole anymore," Alexandra finally said.

"We are so sorry," Poul said.

Alexandra watched as her sweet boy stared at her in disbelief. "Can't see him anymore? But...but what does that mean? Why?"

"We understand you're confused and feeling upset about this," Poul said. "We know how much you loved swimming with him."

Samuel rose from the couch. His eyes were fixated on Alexandra. "So why won't you let me go there anymore? Why won't you let me be happy?"

Alexandra's heart was beating fast in fear. Samuel's pitch-black eyes were staring at her with deep anger.

"Relax, son," Poul said.

"Don't tell me to relax!" he yelled. "It's you, isn't it?" Samuel asked and pointed at Alexandra. "You did this, didn't you? You don't want me to be happy."

Alexandra gasped. "No! No! Samuel. Why would you say such a horrible thing? Of course I didn't do this, it was..."

"I don't care!" Samuel yelled. He grabbed a vase sitting on the end table next to the couch and threw it against the wall, smashing it with a loud crash. Alexandra gasped again. Tears filled her eyes.

Why God? Why did this have to happen? Everything was going so well. Why did you have to ruin it? Is it to punish us?

"I hate you!" Samuel yelled and pointed his finger at her. "You're stupid. You ruin everything!"

Alexandra felt Poul's hand in hers and, as Samuel grabbed a lamp and threw it at her, Poul pulled her out of the room.

65

FEBRUARY 2014

I brought Victor home in my car and tried to help him calm down by singing some of the songs he used to like to hear. I couldn't stop the tears from rolling down my cheeks. Tears of relief that he was safe, tears of fear of what might have happened and tears of anger for what this bastard had put upon me and my family. I thought about all the kinds of revenge I could come up with while driving us home. Once I parked the car in the driveway, I turned in my seat and looked at Victor. He was lying down, staring emptily into the ceiling, whimpering, crying, and shaking.

I tried to fight my tears, but they wouldn't stop. "Victor, buddy. We're home. We're safe."

"Don't touch me," he mumbled. "Don't touch me!"

"No one is going to touch you. Not anymore. I promise you that," I said, my voice breaking. "No one."

But nothing seemed to get through to him. No matter what I said. He had gone into a state of shock or anxiety and I couldn't rip him out of it. All I could do was to give him time. Time and space. But first, I had to get him inside the house somehow and he wasn't responding to anything I said to him. There was only one solution and he wasn't going to like it.

I got out of the car and pulled Victor out of the back seat and carried him back inside, not caring that he was screaming.

"I'm sorry, Victor. I know I promised not to touch you, but I have to get you inside," I said, while tears rolled down my cheeks. I hated to see him like this. It was awful. It was beyond that. It was ghastly.

"Calm down, sweetie. I'm just helping you get inside," I said. "It's all going to be alright. You can play in the backyard with your trees all day if you like."

The talk of his trees seemed to calm him down a little. I managed to get him inside the house and put him on the couch in the living room. My mom came towards me when she heard me enter.

"Oh my God. How is he?"

"In shock, I think." I found a blanket and covered his body. He crumbled up and turned his back to me. "I think we'll let him rest a little. Where is Dad?" I asked, as soon as we had gotten out of the living room.

"He had to go. Something to do with a patient. He told me he's doing a little dentist work on the side. I told him everything you told me on the phone on your way back and, as soon as he knew you were both fine, I told him it was alright if he left. He'll be back later," she said and, suddenly, I spotted something in her eyes I hadn't seen in a long time.

"Will he now? So are you two, all of a sudden, best buddies?" I asked.

"Well. We did spend the night on the couch together. It was really nice. We talked for hours before we fell asleep. It was really nice, Emma. I had forgotten how much I love him, how much I enjoy his company. Ah, what have I been doing with my life, huh?"

"Don't ask me."

"I know. I've been a fool, haven't I? I had this great guy who loved me and I thought I wanted to go out and *live my life*. Well, I tell you Emma, it's all over now. No more running away. I'm going to stay here on the island and see how things turn out with your father."

My eyes almost popped out of my head. That's how it felt. "Really?"

"Yes. It's time for us to grow up, don't you think?"

I chuckled. "Well..."

"Arh, what do you know? You're still so young. You'll go through stuff one day too, you know. Then you'll understand."

"I feel like I'm going through stuff constantly lately," I said, as I exhaled.

"Oh gosh, Emma. I'm so sorry. You must be exhausted. This has been a rough time for you. Let me make you some coffee and maybe something to eat?"

"As long as it is not any of your organic or gluten-free food," I said with a chuckle.

"Scouts' honor," my mom said and held up two fingers in the air.

I opened the door to the kitchen and we both entered, laughing. Then I stopped. What I saw made my heart stop. Maya was sitting at the table with a piece of paper in her hand. Next to her was the empty white envelope.

"Hi, Maya," my mother chirped. "You want something to eat as well?"

Maya lifted her eyes from the paper and stared at me. The look in those eyes was a horrific mixture of deep disappointment and furor.

"What's this?" she asked me.

I walked closer. "I...Maya...I...," I had no idea what to say to her. I hadn't even read the letter myself.

A tear left the corner of her eye. Then she spoke the words that I had dreaded hearing so much.

"Dad is not my real father?"

66

FEBRUARY 2014

"**M**AYA...I..."

"When were you going to tell me?" she interrupted.

"I don't know...I didn't even read the letter yet. I put it in the drawer..."

"Where I found it and saw my name on the envelope. Why would you have such a test taken without my knowledge?"

"Well, I thought there was no need for you to know about this. I mean, if it turned out Michael was your father, then you didn't need to know, right?"

"Did it ever occur to you that maybe I didn't *want* to know this? I have a dad. I don't need someone else, who I've never even heard of. Who is this...Erik Gundtofte? What kind of name is that even? It's stupid. Just like him."

Maya got up from her chair. My mother was looking at us with wide open eyes. "What is going on here, Emma?" she asked. "Michael isn't Maya's father?"

"This is none of your business," I said.

Maya looked at her grandmother. Then she threw herself at

her. My mom hugged her and petted her head, while Maya cried her heart out.

My mother stroked her hair a couple of times. Then Maya turned towards me. "I hate you!" she yelled and grabbed her jacket before she stormed out of the house. I was about to run after her when my mother stopped me.

"Let her blow off steam. She'll probably just go to a friend's house. Don't worry. Give her some space."

I started crying. My mom hugged me. "I've made such a mess of things, Mom. I can't seem to do anything right!"

"There, there. It's going to be alright. Just you wait and see."

"I'm so glad you're here, Mom. I really need you now," I said.

"And I'm not going anywhere."

I sniffled and pulled away from her. I sat on a chair while she prepared food for me. Two pieces of rye bread. One with paté and the other with herrings in curry sauce. My favorite.

"Thanks," I said, while I ate. I had gotten really hungry.

"No problem," she said.

"What are you going to do about Arne?" I asked, in order to think about something else. I was worried about both Maya and Victor now. Morten had called me while I was in the car and said that the bomb wasn't a real bomb. It was a decoy, a fake. The killer hadn't wanted to blow any of us up. He wanted us to be in that situation...much like the one from the train. I was hoping that Morten and his colleagues would finally get a breakthrough in the case today while going through the crime scene at the bank, but my phone had been awfully quiet.

"Well I'll have to break the news to him, won't I?" she asked. "Do the respectable thing and tell him gently that it's over."

"I hope he won't be too heartbroken and pee on our mail or anything," I said.

My mother laughed. "No. He won't do anything like that. He's a good man, Emma. Not that I know how to spot one even though he's been right next to me for years, right?"

I shrugged. "Well, you see him now. And you married him in the first place, didn't you. You just got a little lost along the way. That happens."

"Could you ever see yourself getting together with Michael again?" my mom asked.

I shook my head. "That's different. He has a new wife now and a child. He's leading an entirely new life and hardly even calls to talk to the kids anymore. He's out of the picture. "

"Well, you never know," my mom said and opened a beer for me.

"So, when are you planning on telling Arne?" I asked, as I took a sip. That hit the spot. Herrings and a beer was one of my favorite combinations. It helped me relax a little, as well.

"Well, he usually comes by around noon with the mail, right? I think I'll make him a cup of coffee."

"Give him the right stuff. Or else you'll give him a reason to get really mad," I said with a grin.

67

JANUARY 2008

S amuel managed to trash the entire living room before he locked himself inside of his room and finally went quiet. Alexandra and Poul stayed in their own bedroom until he was done, then snuck downstairs and looked at the damage. Alexandra clapped her hand against her mouth in distress and gasped.

"Oh my God. He's destroyed everything, Poul."

She felt Poul's arm around her. "I know, honey. But they're just things. We'll buy new ones. We knew he wouldn't take it well and, now that he is off his meds, there's nothing to calm him down. He'll get over it."

"You think?"

"He's older now. It's not like before. He just needs to remember the techniques that Ole taught him."

"I don't want to have to send him away again," Alexandra said. "Not now that it has been going so well."

"And we don't have to if he behaves. But I will not have him here if he has more of these tantrums. It's too dangerous with Olivia in the house."

"Samuel would never hurt her. He loves her. Sometimes I think she is the only one who gets him around here."

"He might not mean to, but she could get hit by something he's throwing. You know he can't control it once he takes off like he did tonight. He doesn't think."

Alexandra picked up a broken piece of an old lamp from the floor. "I loved this lamp," she said. "It used to be my grandmother's."

Poul helped her pick up the rest of the pieces and put them in the trash. Then they found a roll of garbage bags and started throwing everything out. Two hours later, they went to bed. It took Alexandra a while to calm down and she cried secretly for about an hour. She didn't want Poul to see how upset she really was, since she was afraid he would start resenting the boy again.

Finally, around midnight, she fell into a deep sleep.

A little later, she was pulled out of her sleep by a strange sound. She opened her eyes and looked at the clock. It was only two a.m. She blinked her eyes. What had woken her? She lifted her head and saw Samuel. He was standing by her bedside, staring at her with a strange look in his eyes.

"Sammy? What are you doing up? It's only two a.m. Did you have a bad dream?"

Suddenly, she was wide awake. She looked down at his PJs and his arm.

Oh my God. Oh my God! He is covered in blood! Is he holding a knife in his hand?

Alexandra sat up and looked at the boy. "Sammy, what are you doing with that knife? What have you done?"

That was when her heart stopped.

Olivia!

She stormed past Samuel into the nursery next door.

Please don't let this be true. Please don't let the blood be Olivia's! Please God! Please, NO!

Alexandra didn't even manage to finish the thought. Once she saw the blood on the crib, she knew it was too late. Samuel was behind her now; she turned and screamed into his face.

"What have you done!!!!?"

In his eyes, she saw nothing. No emotion of any kind. Just pitch blackness. No remorse, no regret, no *I'm sorry, Mom, the voices told me to do this*, no explanation. Nothing.

He opened his mouth and spoke: "You're stupid, Mom."

She barely saw what happened. She only felt the pain from the knife as it sank into her chest and made her heart stop immediately.

68

FEBRUARY 2014

Morten called again to tell me it looked like they might be in luck.

"Looks like our friend have made a mistake," he said. "The security cameras were on the entire time while he placed Victor inside the bank. Well, not all of them, since he managed to shut most of them off, but one was still working; one, I'm guessing, he didn't know about. They had it installed just a week ago."

"That is wonderful news," I exclaimed.

"Yeah. Now we're going through the footage, but so far we haven't been able to see his face properly, since he's wearing a cap."

"No glasses or long hair?" I asked.

"Not this time, no. Maybe that's because we released the sketch of him."

"But you can't see his face properly, huh?"

"No, but at least, so far, we can see him placing Victor and there is no longer any doubt about Victor's innocence. So, you can breathe a little lighter now. It was a wild thing you did to take him home before we had him examined. Be glad you know me, since I managed to talk the officer in charge out of arresting you for destroying evidence."

"I couldn't let them touch Victor anymore. You know how he is. He can't take it. I had to get him out of there."

"I understand, but it took some talking before the officer in charge realized it was okay."

"Thanks," I said.

"No problem," Morten said.

"Now, go back to that footage," I said. "I want that bastard off the streets."

"Yes, ma'am!" Morten said and hung up.

I finished my food and the beer. I walked into the living room to check on Victor. He was sound sleep on the couch. I breathed a sigh of relief. He seemed calm now. That was good. I grabbed my phone and tried to call Maya, but she didn't answer. I sent her another text, telling her I was sorry and to come home so we could talk. I didn't like that she was out there while the killer was still on the loose.

Hopefully, Morten will catch him now.

I wondered about that Ole Knudsen character from the Inn and thought about calling him. I never really got to ask him why he left Hummelgaarden. I thought about just driving out there today to talk to him. I had a feeling he was more closely attached to this entire affair than we had thought at first. I walked back into the kitchen to my mom, who was doing the dishes. It was so nice to have her in the house. She lifted her head and looked out the window.

"There he is," she said and took off her apron. "How do I look?"

"Too good for someone who is about to crush a man's heart."

My mom shrugged. "Well I can't help it. He'll just have to mourn me, right?"

I chuckled. "Right. Good luck."

I found my laptop and placed it on the kitchen table, while

listening to my mother open the front door and call for Arne to come up to the door.

"Poor guy," I mumbled. "He'll never know what hit him."

I googled Ole Knudsen and found the Inn online. Then, I found a newspaper article dating back to 2008.

Employees Escaping Hummelgaarden, was the title. I started reading. *Yet another of Hummelgaarden's counselors left the institution yesterday because of a disagreement with the management at City Hall.*

"It is most unfortunate that Ole has chosen to leave us, but that's his choice," a social worker named Marianne Moeller was quoted as saying.

Marianne Moeller? Wasn't that the woman who was found killed in her souvenir shop? Could hardly be a coincidence, could it? I continued, as I heard my mother talk to Arne and try to persuade him to come in for coffee, while he tried to explain that he was working and way too busy.

"I can't live with the choices that they're making at City Hall anymore," Ole Knudsen was quoted as saying. *"It's not human. The system is broken. They destroyed that family."*

Family? What family? I kept reading and got my answer.

Earlier this week, a family tragedy occurred in a home here on Fanoe. A young boy named Samuel Holm killed his mother and younger sister with a knife in the middle of the night. Samuel was one of Ole Knudsen's patients, who he took care of in his free time by going swimming with him, since there was no room for Samuel at the institution. The city stopped Ole's treatment of Samuel, since he wasn't allowed to do it outside of work hours.

"Of course, I blame myself," Ole told the paper. *"I was doing a great job with the boy. I shouldn't have let City Hall stop me. I should have left this place much earlier and still seen Samuel. Maybe this tragedy wouldn't have happened."*

Now, Ole Knudsen is planning on opening up an Inn in the middle of the island.

"I really can't see how this is something you can blame anyone for, tragedies happen all the time. We can't blame ourselves every time, another social worker named Tine Solvang said.

I leaned back in my chair feeling that aha-moment. "So Ole is mad at the system. Ole decides to do something about it, to change it?"

My mom finally managed to get Arne inside the house. I heard them walk into the living room. I decided to let them have their privacy, hoping they wouldn't wake up Victor. I looked at the article again and again. A big picture of Ole Knudsen stared back at me.

Could it really be him?

"If the shoes fits..."

My mom entered the kitchen. She looked stressed out. "He'll be fine, Mom," I said. "He's a big boy."

She found two cups and poured coffee into them. "I know. I just really don't like to have to do this. What are you up to?"

"I think I might have found the identity of The Caring Killer."

"Really? That's interesting. Better tell Morten, then. Now, if you'll excuse me, I have to break up with my boyfriend."

My mom left the room with a tray between her hands carrying cups and a plate of cookies. I chuckled and shook my head. Crazy old woman. Living the life of a teenager.

I decided to dig a little deeper on the story and googled *family tragedy on Fanoe Island.*

Up came a lot of articles from 2008. I decided to open one and read through it, then looked at the picture. It was a nice picture of the family before the tragedy. Underneath it, the text said:

The happy family before the tragedy. Only the dad survived Samuel Holm's nighttime attack on his own family. Poul Arne Holm testified against his son today. Samuel Holm is under the age of consent and will probably be sentenced to spending the rest of his teen-age years in a closed institution.

I froze. I stared at the picture, and especially at the father's face that I suddenly recognized. For seconds, I refused to believe it. Then I read the text again.

"Poul *Arne* Holm?"

I lifted my head and stared at the kitchen door that my mother had just gone through.

Oh my God.

69

FEBRUARY 2014

I sprang through the kitchen door and into the living room, slamming the door open.

"Emma?" my mother said, startled. "What are you doing?"

I searched for Victor and saw, to my relief, that he was still sleeping on the couch.

"Emma?" my mother said again. "We're kind of in the middle of something here."

I tried hard to control my breath. I stared at Arne, sitting on my couch, holding a cup of coffee between his hands. He was smiling at me.

"Well hello there, Emma. You seem upset. Are you upset?"

"He," I said and pointed. "You..."

Arne tilted his head. "Now Emma, you know it's not polite to point, don't you? I think your mom must have taught you better than that."

My mother was suspecting that something was wrong. She looked at Arne, then back at me.

"What are you trying to say?"

"The Caring Killer. He's the killer. The one who has been harassing us."

"Excuse me?" my mother said. She looked like she was trying to decide whether to laugh or cry.

"No, Ulla. It's alright," Arne said, with a creepily calm voice. "Let her talk."

"You did this to us? You did all of this to us?" I said, still pointing my shaking finger at him. "Why?"

Arne sipped his coffee with stoic calmness. Then he sucked his teeth. "Well, if you must know, I like to play games," he said the last word with a grin.

"You're crazy," I said.

Arne tilted his head. "Well it depends on your definition of crazy now, doesn't it, my dear? The word crazy isn't really a psychological term now is it? You know just as well as I do that there are many degrees to craziness or mental illness. You've tried it, haven't you Emma? You've been through it. Been through the system. Tried to fight for your son. Tried to get the help you needed, but just kept running that pretty face of yours against a wall again and again, didn't you? Well, there is your answer. That's why I chose you. I knew you would understand. You, of all people, would know what I wanted. See, I've been watching you, Emma. Ever since you moved here, I have delivered mail to your house and followed your life. I knew about Victor. That's why you were perfect. That and the fact that you write books about your life. I was kind of hoping you'd write about this, as well. Maybe get all the details about how badly mentally ill people are treated in our society, as well. Really stir up people and maybe make them want things to change. Say, are there more of those cookies? They're simply delicious."

Arne leaned over the table and took another cookie. I was shaking in anger. This creep had been watching me?

"How?" I asked. "How did you do all those awful things to these people?"

"I knew them. I knew everything about them. I was their mailman, remember? A mailman knows everything. He knows all of your little secrets. The mailman knows everyone, sees everyone, but very few people see him when he secretly opens your mail and glues it back again before he delivers it to you. He knows if your mother has died and the lawyer writes to you, he knows what illnesses you suffer from when the doctor or the county sends you letters about it, talking about disability income and so on. He even knows the codes to the security system in the bank, since it has just been changed and sent it in a registered letter to the manager. Everybody trusts the mailman, don't they? Taking Victor was probably the easiest part. Your father was asleep, so I could walk right in through the front door that he hadn't locked. I had left your mother at the restaurant, telling her I had somewhere important to be. Telling her I had promised my old mother I'd stop by and wish her Happy Valentine's Day. I sedated Victor while he was sleeping and carried him out to the car. There was no one in the streets except from some weird guy in a black suit that I saw cross the street and hide in your yard. But, he didn't seem to care about me."

"Why did you hurt Ole Knudsen if he was the only person who ever helped you and your son?"

"I wanted you to meet him. I wanted you to connect the dots so you could write my story. The story of the system that killed my family. Ole plays an important role. I never hurt him, though. I just tied him up and led you to him."

Arne chewed and washed the cookie down with coffee, then he looked at me again. "See the thing is, Emma. In the beginning, I blamed my son for what happened. For a long time, I blamed him, but as time went by, I realized he wasn't the problem. The system was what screwed everything up. There was one place, one person that could help my son, but they weren't allowed to. Because of rigid rules and regulations. Well those rules and regulations killed my family. Those social workers killed my family. So, I killed them.

But that wasn't quite enough. I wanted to kill the system as well. Save Hummelgaarden and change the system. That was my plan. And I wanted you to help me. I wanted you to see the unfairness. No, it was more than that; I wanted you to feel it. How did it feel to stand there in the bank with your son when everyone thought he was dangerous? It wasn't a nice feeling was it? To have to explain to people that he was simply scared. Explain that he didn't respond like *normal* people would in a situation like this. Wasn't fun, was it? Well now you know what it feels like. Now you can write about it."

"I won't write about this. I'm not giving you that pleasure," I said through gritted teeth.

Arne took another cookie and dipped it in his coffee. "Well that's just too bad, Emma. 'Cause then I'll have to kill all of you."

As he said the words, he lifted his coffee cup and threw the burning hot coffee at my mother's face.

She screamed. Then I screamed. Victor woke up and screamed and then there was someone else who was screaming. Someone jumping out from the closet in my living room with a long sword in his hand, dressed all in black.

Startled, I looked at the black ninja in my living room as he jumped in front of me, sounding like a kid playing.

"What the hell?" I said.

"It's burning. It's burning!" I heard my mother scream.

"Don't touch me! Don't touch me!" I heard Victor scream.

"Who the hell is this?" I heard Arne ask.

I had no idea.

The ninja looked at the scene, then turned towards me. "Emma Frost. I'm here to save you. This is my mission."

Then he lifted his sword in the air with the words:

"I'm sorry Emma, but you've been way too fearful the last several days. It's time to set you free from your fears. The voice told me to save you from yourself. You can thank me later."

Before I could react, he stabbed the sword into my stomach. I gasped as I saw it go through and the blood started pouring out. I bent over and leaned on the wall. I watched the blood gush to the floor. I started getting dizzy and had moments of blackout. I fell to the ground, just as I heard the front door open and Morten's voice yell.

"This is the police. Everybody down on the floor!"

After that, everything went black.

EPILOGUE
FEBRUARY 2014

I woke up in a hospital bed. Morten was sitting next to me, holding my hand. His eyes were red when he looked at me. He'd been crying.

"Hey," I said with a weak voice.

"Emma! You're awake!" he said and got up.

"Yeah. Feels like I'm still in a dream though."

"Oh, how happy I am to see you again," he said and kissed my hand. "You had us all worried there."

"What happened?"

"We got them. Both Poul Arne Holm and Anders Samuelsen are locked up now. Don't worry about them."

"Anders Samuelsen? The guy from the coffin? He was the ninja?"

"I know, it's weird. Apparently, he lost it after what happened to him. Didn't take his medicine. We don't know all the details yet, but it is a very strange story, I'll tell you that much."

"You came right in time, huh? My knight in shining armor. How did you know?"

"I saw the mailman's face on the video footage. I remembered seeing him at your house that day you received the head in the mail. I tried to call you, but you didn't answer. I decided to drive to your house to make sure you were alright and that was when I noticed that his postal bike was parked outside your house. The rest is history. Luckily, with a good ending."

"My mom and Victor. How are they?"

"Victor is with your dad at the house. Your mom...well, it doesn't look good."

I rose in the bed and felt dizzy. "What doesn't look good? Is she...?"

"Well, it's only her skin that got burned and she'll be fine, but the warm coffee kind of ruined her face a little."

I fell back in the bed. "Really? How bad is it?"

"Don't know yet. They've taken skin from her leg to cover it."

"Oh, that sounds bad. Guess Botox and facelifts won't help her this time."

"No. But, at least she has a guy who loves her. Your dad has been so nice to her while she's been in the hospital. He sent her a hundred red roses today. And balloons. Her room is filled with balloons."

I chuckled lightly. It hurt my wound. "I hope he won't get his heart crushed again," I said.

"He's a good man, your dad."

"So are you," I said.

"I still owe you a dinner," he said and kissed me. "By the way, I thought of something while waiting for you to wake up. I don't know if it's the solution, but maybe it could help."

"What's that?"

"With Victor. I know you've been thinking a lot about how to help him and keep him in school. Well, I thought maybe Ole could help him? I mean he doesn't work for the city anymore, so he can do whatever he wants. He's been wanting to get back to work with kids again, so maybe it's an idea?"

"That's a great idea," I said. "I'll call him right away."

"Better wait till you're well," Morten said and kissed me again. "By the way, there is someone here to see you."

"Who's that?"

Morten left and, soon after, a voice filled the room.

"Mom?"

Maya stuck her face inside.

"Maya, dear. I'm so happy to see you. How are you?"

She stopped by the end of the bed. Her eyes avoided mine.

"It's okay, Maya. You're entitled to be angry."

She nodded, while still looking down. "I'm glad you're better."

"Me too. Hopefully, I'll be home soon. Has grandpa taken good care of you?"

Maya nodded. "Listen, Mom. There's something I want to tell you."

"Sure. Anything, sweetheart."

Finally, she looked up and our eyes met. I smiled. I missed her.

"I want to go live with Dad."

She didn't wait for my answer. As soon as she'd finished the sentence, she turned around and left.

The End

———

Want to know what happens next? Get the next novel in the Emma Frost Mystery series here: http://www.amazon.com/Tweedledum and Tweedledee

AFTERWORD

Dear Reader,

Thank you for purchasing *Peek-a-Boo, I See You*. I hope you enjoyed it and want to get the rest in the series.

Don't forget to check out my other books if you haven't already read them. Just follow the links below. And don't forget to leave reviews, if you can.

Take care,
Willow

Tired of too many emails? Text the word: "willowrose" to 31996 to sign up to Willow's VIP text List to get a text alert with news about New Releases, Giveaways, Bargains and Free books from Willow.

ABOUT THE AUTHOR

The Queen of Scream aka Willow Rose is a #1 Amazon Best-selling Author and an Amazon ALL-star Author of more than 80 novels.

She writes Mystery, Paranormal, Romance, Suspense, Horror, Supernatural thrillers, and Fantasy.

Willow's books are fast-paced, nail-biting page-turners with twists you won't see coming.

Several of her books have reached the Kindle top 20 of ALL books in the US, UK, and Canada.

She has sold more than four million books all over the world.

Willow lives on Florida's Space Coast with her husband and two daughters. When she is not writing or reading, you will find her surfing and watch the dolphins play in the waves of the Atlantic Ocean.

———

To be the first to hear about new releases and bargains—from Willow Rose—sign up below to be on the VIP List. (I promise not to share your email with anyone else, and I won't clutter your inbox.)

- GO HERE TO SIGN UP TO BE ON THE VIP LIST :

http://bit.ly/VIP-subscribe

Tired of too many emails? Text the word: "willowrose" to 31996 to sign up to Willow's VIP text List to get a text alert with news about New Releases, Giveaways, Bargains and Free books from Willow.

Cover design by Juan Villar Padron,
https://juanjjpadron.wixsite.com/juanpadron

Special thanks to my editor Janell Parque
http://janellparque.blogspot.com/

————

To be the first to hear about new releases and bargains from Willow Rose, sign up below to be on the VIP List. (I promise not to share your email with anyone else, and I won't clutter your inbox.)

- Tap here to sign up to be on the VIP LIST -

Tired of too many emails? Text the word: "willowrose" to 31996 to sign up to Willow's VIP text List to get a text alert with news about New Releases, Giveaways, Bargains and Free books from Willow.

Follow Willow Rose on BookBub:

 Follow me on BookBub

Connect with Willow online:
Facebook
Twitter
GoodReads
willow-rose.net
madamewillowrose@gmail.com

Lightning Source UK Ltd.
Milton Keynes UK
UKHW012236060223
416577UK00009B/623/J